Time's Oldest Daughter tells an impossible story of the world before the world, the time before time, when none of the categories we use to think with yet existed. Lyons spins out the intertwined beginnings of semiotics and physics, from the first separation of subject and object in language (Satan's separation from God) to the necessary co-presence of matter and time in the universe (as Satan and his daughter Sin fall into the world of physical and temporal forces and order them through their experience). The primary agent who navigates the ongoing process of a creation that includes quarks and photons, bacteria and algae is female, and infinitely older than Eve: Sin, born in heaven before the fall, the shadow that fell as Satan stepped away from God. John Milton, Sylvia Plath, Stanley Fish and Julia Kristeva would all recognize themselves in this book, though none of them wrote it. Lyons did, and her remarkable rethink of *Paradise Lost* in the person of Sin, Satan's daughter, struggling to find a place for her son, Death, in creation is wonderfully and determinedly original.

—Sarah Tolmie, author of
The Stone Boatmen and *Two Travelers*

Time's Oldest Daughter

Time's Oldest Daughter

Susan W. Lyons

Seattle

Aqueduct Press, PO Box 95787
Seattle, WA 98145-2787
www.aqueductpress.com

ISBN: 978-1-61976-105-6
Library of Congress Control Number: 2016962864
10 9 8 7 6 5 4 3 2 1

Cover and Book Design by Kathryn Wilham

Front Cover: Painting: Die Sünde, Franz von Stuck, 1893

Printed in the USA by Thomson Shore, Inc.

Dear reader, this book would not have reached you without the fresh and perceptive eyes of my students, colleagues & editors, family, and friends. My deep thanks to them and to you for spending time with this story.

In the beginning, God created Heaven and Earth.
—Genesis 1:1

Out of thy head I sprung. Amazement seized
All the host of heaven; back they recoiled afraid
At first, and called me Sin, . . .
—John Milton. Paradise Lost (2.758-60)

$e=mc^2$

—Albert Einstein

Engendering Sin

As I was being born, I was being raped.

As I was being raped, I was becoming a mother.

These I owe to you, Lucifer, Bringer of Light.

Really.

Thanks, Daddy.

Thank you so much.

Before Time, there is being. After Time, there is becoming.

Of course, since at that Time you didn't know about Time, how would you know about "before" or "after," let alone "being" or "becoming," when you decided to step away from the perfect composition of elements called God? You would have had to have known about Time in order to know about being and becoming, right? Even the terms "at that Time" and "would have had to have known" are locked into an ordering of events, a narrative, if you will. And narratives require multiples of words like "then" or "now," "before" or "after," "here" or "there"—if for no other reason than to keep Time and narrative from charging off in an entirely disorderly fashion.

Toward entropy.

Into chaos.

See, Daddy? I already digress. It's these damned words, you see. They(it) slip(s) and slide(s) under the strain of description. They fracture; they dis-integrate. But still, they are all I have.

Before Time there was just this one Word, this endless whoopee of praise in a place that was not yet a place and a Time that was not yet in Time. All that is/was/will be forever exists/existed/will exist in an eternal presence that is/was/will be eternally present.

So, Sire, just what was it that were you thinking as you stepped away?

You were thinking that praise without beginning or ending gets old after a while. And yet you couldn't even articulate that, because in the eternal present there is no word for "old," let alone "after a while." It is—they are—all together and altogether God. But if the endless love, perfume, radiance, sound, light, and joyJoyJOY bring on the celestial migraine, I can understand why you'd want to step out of the roaring dazzle for relief, even *moment*arily. Into a darker, cooler, quieter, restful *moment*. And the notion that you can even conceive of "endless" or "momentarily" suggests that you can also conceive of stepping away.

So, you are thinking about your celestial migraine brought on by undifferentiated bliss within an eternal presence that is eternally present. I get it. You conceive of stepping away. And because you can conceive of it, you do it. Just as you conceive me, whatever "me" comes to mean.

You take a step back, resisting a slight tug, a light brush with Time, you could say, and you step away, separate and distinct, into your own "space," let's call it. In that space, the light, the sound, the noise, and the smell have diminished, and in that "have diminished" (Ah, present *perfect* tense!), you notice "before," when you were all together, and "after," when you're not. The migraine now pulses in Time.

And in that slightly diminished light you now see a shadow. Your shadow. Your very own shadow, Daddy. That would be me. And your very own shadow marks the alluring, not to say seductive length between you and whatever remains of God. You have limned distance. You claim that shadow, me, your first follower, for yourself. Nobody else's but your own.

"She, a shadow he," you call me.

You have engendered me even as you've begotten me. How clever! Of course what you might have not noticed in all the excitement is that you've also gendered your own self.

You-who? You-he. Me-she. Yoo-hoo!

Well.

And speaking of excitement. Not only have you stepped away and made a shadow, you've figured out how to keep her (me) for yourself. All for yourself. Not for them. Not for God. Just for you. "Shhhhhh . . . little shadow. You're mine, all mine," you think as you rape me, impregnate me, and pin me underfoot.

Stepping away. What a brilliant notion. Bravo! But there's more. In the shadow made by your decision to step out of the glare, you see that you yourself have discovered an independent and distinct point of view, a singular perspective in which, away from the dazzle, you see a puffy face, a little jowly, a little smug, crimson in the afterglow of all that singing and adoration. You see a hard gaze and a small mouth pursed in sudden displeasure. You see pupils widened in shock, surrounded by golden irises.

This is what you've been yahooing to? This is what all the Godly fuss has been about? You take another step back, and then another, creating more distance, a larger shadow, defining still more "before" and "after."

"Hey, you out there," you shout, words shooting off like sparks. "Come over here and take a look at this." A few— Belial, Mammon, Moloch, and the more restless or unstable of the elementals—join you. With their departure, the praise of the spheres shudders, then falters, clangs, and halts.

And what's left of God stutters a few new words of their own. "Huh? What? Why? Who?"

You respond with a far more articulate question of your own: "How can I see my own light," you ask, "in all your razzle-dazzle?"

"Well, Lucifer Light Bringer," they reply, in voices that begin chorally but will shortly diverge. "It's not about *your* light—it's about your light and praise bringing the greater glory to all of us, to We." But even as God ponder(s) the use of "I" and "your" when all previously has been We and Our, God realize(s) that Word has fractured into words, so that one word leads to another, and then another. Soon numbers will be needed to track them, and they will grow increasingly argumentative, inharmonious, discordant.

As further words are invented and exchanged, additional points of view accumulate and diverge. How can that be? Remember your original decision to step back and admire the shortest distance between the origin and the point you created? It's a line, and the line gives you your own singular point of view, but once you've invited others to step away from God and they've joined you, they too exist in space, but not in your space, because it's already yours, right, Daddy? Just like I am your shadow, not theirs? And so they have to find their *own* distance, not yours. And, oh dear, this creates yet more division. In inscribing their own lines and spaces, they fracture and multiply points into lines and planes and angles and perspectives. And, frankly, although I hate to mention this, Daddy, just as you did, now so do they choose to occupy space as mass.

And soon there's massive pushing and shoving for the best space from which to manifest their own personal points of view. There's Moloch, glowering high from behind your left wing. Yes, Daddy, you do now manifest a pair of magnificent wings, along with long arms, big fists, and sharp elbows with which to claim and protect your space. Belial crouches beneath the shelter of your right wing, peering out. Mammon, distracted by a now-visible glitter of pavement—after all, now that you have mass you might as well have *something* to stand on—tries to shove you aside to better see his own vision of a celestial floor of lapis grouted in gold. But you're not letting him into your manifest space, are you? You're standing your ground.

And now as push comes to shove, the very space itself expands and heats up, roiling from the force of Mammon's impulse over Time to displace you against the massive inertia of your own determination to keep your own place, your own space, your own property, your own domain, intact.

And what am I doing underneath all this pushing and shoving, Daddy, trampled underfoot as you compete for prime real estate? I'm doing some pushing of my own. Sire, I'm increasing your domain. I'm giving you a son, a grandchild.

Death is on his way.

The Falling Out

"Well, perhaps the first order of business is to sort ourselves out," says God to themselves.

"Sort ourselves out?" they respond.

"I/We don't see how we can possibly maintain the perfect present in a dimensional world," God says. "We have to change, and we have to understand Time. This splitting and fracturing of the eternal into before, now, and later. This business of words, and, in particular, pronouns. This concept of space, and property. What have they to do with composed and perfect harmony? Once we were only We; then we were you and I; soon, I suppose, if not already, we'll be they."

You're the first to speak out. "I see nothing odd about singularity," you say. "Talk about odd—

"There once was a presence called God, whose ideas of perfection were odd.

"They stayed altogether with no sense of wherever like so many peas in a pod."

"What are peas?" asks Raphael.

"Did you just speak in rhythm, Lucifer?" asks Gabriel, who is discovering a singular pleasure in sound.

"And doggerel?" asks Polyhymnia, less approvingly.

"Ignore him, Gabriel," says Michael, irritated beyond measure at Lucifer's behavior.

"What is 'him'?" asks Mnemosyne "I remember nothing about a 'him.'"

"I invented 'him'!" you say proudly. "And I invented 'her,' too.

"I made me a shadow called 'daughter,' and I am the father who wrought her.

"So my shadow's a she, and yours truly a he, as well as the world's foremost author!"

"Are limericks, a shadow, and gendered sex the best you can come up with?" asks Michael. "We can do so much better than that, can't we?" the elemental asks, appealing to God.

"Michael, am I sharpening your competitive instincts?" you sneer.

"I'll show you sharp!" says Michael, and even as he speaks, a burnished sword manifests. All stare, but Michael stares the hardest.

"Stop. See how we are dis-integrating even as we speak," says God. The sword shimmers and dissipates. "We fragment from our former wholeness. We decompose."

"Well then, let's compose ourselves," says Calliope.

"This is change. This is choice," says Raphael, gently.

"This is difference; this is disagreeable," mutters Michael.

"What's wrong with difference?" you ask. "What's wrong with disagreeable?

"*I* love this new living in space. Being singular puts me in *my* place.

"*I*'ll make a new name, while staking a claim that Heaven will soon be *my* base."

"Heaven?" asks God. "What is Heaven?"

"Have you not noticed, God, that the ones who have stepped away now have a place of their own to stand on? Is that not Heaven?"

"Thank God Lucifer's not speaking in rhyme anymore," murmurs Polyhymnia to Gabriel. Gabriel doesn't reply. He is studying you, Daddy, or at least how your hands tap restlessly as you speak.

"Names, names, names, ..." God says, observing the expressions of the several new manifestations of that which once comprised wholeness but who now speak in increasingly discordant voices. "First there was Time, then distance and space, and words, and still more words. And now names. New names like Heaven, and, now, that which is not Heaven." God turns the gaze to Lucifer. "We understand, Lucifer. You are—were—a light bringer, it's true, but you added it into our greater glory. Alone, singularly, as you yourself say, you show only a brief, flaring, quickly extinguished light. You are easily bored, as we all can see. You are making a new name for yourself? Very well, then. We will call you by your elemental name, Phosphorus, for you are volatile and reactive."

"Volatile? Reactive? Me?" you sputter.

"And self-igniting and toxic, apparently. Are you sure you and the others—whether you call yourselves Mammon, Belial, Lilith, and Moloch; or Plutonium, Antimony, Uranium, and Sulfur—don't want to return to wholeness? See how Francium is already decomposing under the influence of Time." Everyone looks. It is true. Uranium rushes to recover the remains.

You flare with brilliant indignation. "Stay with you? You with your smug, self-righteous face? Why would I stay with *you*?" you sizzle.

God says, "We had not yet taken on faces when you stepped away. The face you saw was yours, was *your own* reflection—all yours, *yours alone*—that *you* saw."

You are stunned, Daddy. Simply stunned. You study the multiple facets, faces, now, of God. "Why didn't you tell me?" you whisper.

"Would you have listened?" Michael asks.

"It's all your fault!!" you shout at God, at Michael, at who-ever will listen. "You owe me! That wasn't what I wanted at all! What I want is...I want my own...I want my own...!"

"You want your own 'what'?" asks God.

"I want what you have."

"You can't," says God. "You can't because you have already chosen to manifest your own space and Time and so we are no longer what we were."

"Oh yes I can," you say. "And I will."

"Oh will you?" shouts Michael, and Time erupts, pro-pelling the story onward as further words are exchanged, points of view accumulate and diverge, and the spaces be-tween the elementals enlarge and boil. No more sorting the words out into strophe or antistrophe, Daddy. Just catas-trophe. Time whirls and stumbles over the present, veers toward the potential. As it brushes past, you feel a force generating the future. In the meanTime, further challeng-es are issued. A blow is struck. Violence escalates. Armies are formed. A charge is led. Weapons of mass punishment are employed. Pain is introduced. Defeat is demonstrated. Winners and losers are declared.

Then, Daddy, you argue about the declaration of "loser" as well as the slave-name Phosphorus, so God, over the objections of Michael and Ares, lets you choose your own name. Those who might have thought you'd lost your spark in the aftermath of the great falling out soon see otherwise. "You know, God," you say. "I really feel as though I have done you all a great service in introducing you to change and variety, along with manifest mass and physical forces."

"And fear and pain and weariness," mutters Michael.

You ignore that cheap remark. "As the fearless leader who dared declare independence against the tyranny of..."

"Joy?" chimes Calliope.

"Unity?" suggests Raphael.

"Against the tyranny of interruption!" you snap. "I am the most honorable and independent Adversary! And so I declare myself the Other. I am S-T-N, Satanas, ha-Satan, Satan! It's a name that's dashing. It's singular. It's real. It's me!"

"Dashing," echoes Inanna, who saw you dashing for the rear lines not so long ago.

But you are already thinking about the glory accumulating around your exploits: Time, space, place, sex, words, points of view, war. Perhaps an epic narrative could do it justice, especially accompanied by some sort of radiance around your singularity. A halo? A crown? A crown of massy gold? But, then, who would hear your story or see your glory if you are the only Other?

"Yes. From now on, call me Satan," you say. "And call me also relieved to be free of this tedious togetherness. Now that I've experienced the magnificence of my singularity, I have no desire to return to a hive mentality. I invented Time, distance, space, mass, and point of view, and I'm entitled to all of them.

"I want my own domain. But," you add graciously, remembering that you desire others to see and appreciate your singularity, "anyone who feels the same way I do may choose to join me." Several of the elements sidle over and stay. Potassium comes, and goes, and comes, and goes, and comes. Carbon watches, bemused. Why choose sides anyway? Why *either or*? Why not *both and*?

The lines eventually settle into two ragged sides. "Everyone has chosen? You've all sorted yourselves out?" God asks. "You're sure?" Potassium scurries Home and resumes its position next to Sodium. God waits until all is still. "Very well, then. Satan!" God thunders. "You want a little distance? You want some perspective? You want a distinctive point of view? Take them. We'll give you all the Time and space and distance you want. All for your own!"

"You mean my own domain?"

"Yes, all for you and yours."

"As far away from you as I can get?"

"Yes. As far away from us as you can possibly get. You may go to Hell. You may all go to Hell."

The Fallout

"Hell," you think to yourself. "If it's away from them, how bad can it be?"

You and they—the other Others (others but not, of course, singularly Other, like you, Daddy)—fall, out of that previously dimensionless place Time, fracturing place from Time, and inscribing distance between places measured in Time—nine days and nine nights, if you decide to keep count, and eventually, you do—keep count that is—because as terrifying as the fall is, at first it's also exhilarating. Faster and faster you go.

"How fast am I falling?" you ask yourself, curious about the extent of your new domain. "How much of this space is mine? How fast am I falling at any moment? How big is my space now? What's my speed?" It's all happening so fast, you think. How thrilling! There you were, Daddy, hanging in an endless suspension of joy, well, forever, it seemed, and now here you are. Wherever and whenever here is, of course. And here does seem to change so quickly into there, and there, and there. But you'll sort it all out. Just as God did.

An exhilarating free fall, you'll call it, because you're finally, you think to yourself, free of that boring conformity. In fact, you think to yourself, it's really a fortunate fall as well as a free fall, because you're gaining independence for you and your colleagues.

You're accelerating, Daddy. How exhilarating! Are you falling faster?

Falling forever?

Falling eternally?

Oddly, now the faster you go, the more slowly Time seems to pass. If you go fast enough, can you slow Time to a standstill? Manufacture your own eternity?

Your shadow, little old me, along with your son/grandson, has fled before you, far and away into uncharted territory. You look around at your remaining fellow fallers. "Fallers?" you ask yourself and you answer, "No! 'Followers.'" Yes, "Followers." Who needs independence when you can have followers?

But then, pain strikes in waves now, not pulses, far worse than your celestial migraine, far more durable than the inconvenient blow that little Abdiel inflicted, even more terrible than that lucky swipe Michael managed to get in. (You weren't looking, that's all.) Alas, this mass that you've acquired, the mass that allowed you to define your own space, is apparently falling right along with you, as well as the mountains, munitions, infernal battle engines, and other detritus of the Dis-integration dumped when you and your followers fled out of God's "domain," I guess you'll have to call it now.

And your collective masses, yes, *collective* masses, seem to be attracting each other in a hideously repulsive sort of way. The gravity of this event momentarily escapes you, but the force of the collisions does not.

Yes.

Pain strikes.

Your new-found words flee in shock.

You have collided with a howitzer that tumbles, along with the rest of your infernal devices and their waste, down with you and the other losers. (Oops, Daddy. Not losers. Followers.) You bounce, careen into a thick path of sorry trash, each collision racking the senses of your newly manifest and now apparently infinitely tormentable fleshy mass: sand, boiling oil, AK-47s, phosphates, battering rams, trebuchets, bazookas, ammonia, mustard gas, smog, gamma rays, dart guns, hollow points, crossbows, syringes, dirty bombs, cyanide, the pox, dandruff, ash, napalm, dengue, dust, earth, air, decrepitude, hunger, fire, shit, fleas, age, and the stink of impending mortality.

The filth is unspeakable.

Cold and heat and erosion and Time and pain burn and consume you.

Time slows as you gather mass but then speeds up as your fall decays.

Your newly acquired vocabulary and flesh decompose.

You disarticulate.

God gazes at the mess you make as you fall. Just look at all the garbage you're leaving in your wake! But God is nothing if not environmentally aware and has already started detoxifying and recycling the debris: sorting out light from darkness, water from land, fire from air, clay from dust, fish from fowl, into a perfectly reusable new creation.

But, Satan, when you fell, were you expecting pain to accompany you? That initial migraine that you imagined? Abdiel's blow? Michael's thrust? Could you feel pain throbbing and banging in the new reality of the harsh wind shrieking through your flailing but useless wings? Did you realize as you tumbled through Chaos that you would begin to bend and twist and tear? That your massless shadow would flee before you into the unimaginable distance? That friction and your resistance would slow you down, heat you up, and scatter you into entropy? That it's the gravity of your own decision that pulls you as far away from God as you can get?

A Genesis

"What a mess," said Ge, on her hands and knees scrubbing the radioactives and neutralizing the toxics leftover from the Dis-integration. Quarks everywhere. Particles slithered about, defying her efforts to locate their position so she could tidy them up. "Damn space," she said to herself.

"Don't forget to ionize the phosphates, sulfates, and nitrates," said Raphael, who was discovering a strong preference for supervising.

She looked up. "A little help, here?"

Raphael said, "I would, but I just washed my wings, and they're still drying." It shrugged to display a shimmering ripple of feathers.

"Hmm," said Ge. "I bet they are." She smiled as she scooped up a refractory photon and handed it to Iris, who set it carefully into a prism where it winked and shimmered.

"Why are we manifesting hands, knees, and wings anyway?" asked Michael. "Do we need them?"

"As I recall, Michael, you've become quite fond of holding and polishing that shiny sword you summoned for battle. And you need hands for that," Gabriel said, as he fingered a hollow brass tube originally engineered by Hephaestus as a bazooka, but that Gabriel himself had modified to herald battle charges. "Besides, you're ethereal. If you don't like your mass, transform it."

"Her? She? Him? Her? It?" asked Apollo. "Who or what is manifesting all these personal pronouns, anyway? And why?"

"We are," said God. "We like the variety."

"But it was Satan who first used personal pronouns," said Raphael.

"Yes, but that doesn't mean we shouldn't continue. Satan was part of us," God said. "And he could be again, if he chooses to come Home before he decays altogether. Of course we've taken a different direction, creating a world that will naturally inhabit Time itself. We've gone organic."

Ge beamed with joy at the great Garden they'd created. "Yes," she said. "We nudged another oxygen onto carbon monoxide and married two hydrogens to an oxygen, with splendid results. We sorted out light from dark, heat from cold, water from earth from air from fire, carbon from silicon. We crafted metals, gases, liquids, and the sublime ability to transform from one state to another."

"Like us," said Proteus.

"Like us," agreed God. "And we made more complex forms that bond through sharing and complementary attractions."

"Too bad Satan didn't think of that," said Inanna, who had admired the elemental's energy, if not his fizzle.

God resumed. "We've repurposed all manner of matter and energy so that they will not get lost but can transform in Time from one to the other and back again."

Ge, pinning down a wriggling quantum, lifted her finger carefully, only to discover that the particle had once again vanished. "Damn Time," she muttered.

God laughed, a booming laugh that echoed in newly manifest ears with much of the joyJoyJOY that had so provoked Satan. "Well, yes. I suppose one might feel that way, at first. But Time will sort itself out."

"Really?" asked Raphael.

"More than just 'really,'" said God. "We have created in Time that which Time enhances. To beauty we have added variety and appetite."

Zeus and Mnemosyne glanced hungrily at each other and away.

"We have shaped photons into particles and waves that in Time and space physically manifest refractions as well as reflections of light, which is itself a Time traveler. We have added color."

Iris beamed.

"To the percussion of the Basso Profundo we have added rhythm, tempo, loudness, softness, timbre, and tones; strings and reeds and brass. We have added voice and sound."

Gabriel nodded approval.

"We have added taste and smell: aromas of honey and vanilla, odors of garlic, mustard, fresh-hot bread." The scent of lemons carried on a warm breeze, and all—elementals and primordials alike—murmured with pleasure at the sensations.

"And, of course, there are our children, undifferentiated now but soon to grow in Time into their own individual fullness."

"I hope not like Satan and his wretched daughter/wife," said Michael.

"She who cried when born? A cry that Lucifer took as pleasure but that she made in pain and anguish? And loneliness? And fear? Satan's first follower? No. Lucifer conceived Sin out of impulse and raped her out of avarice and vanity. We have conceived our own children with loving care: carbon and hydrogen because they play so well with others, and oxygen for its affinity with Time. The volatiles and reactives we still keep for spark, but they are incorporated sparingly."

"'Loving care'? 'Incorporated'?" asked Ge.

"When love and free will composed us, we were wholly and entirely without domain. Free will let us choose to remain together. Or to leave. We chose to stay. Satan and his followers chose to leave. As we disintegrated, love itself split and fractured, falling into the cracks between we and you; us and them.

"Love can fill those cracks, or we can form new connections and bonds in different ways. As for incorporation, we will put ourselves into our creations, and therefore bring our creations into ourselves. As for aging, some of us will be newer—younger—than others. We will bequeath wisdom through Time, experience, and growth to these younger members. They will bring freshness and variety to us. We will be necessary to each other, and we will connect across the spaces. From Satan's descendance will come our descendants, and we will call them our children, and they will grow up in Time and experience. We will be family."

Apollo nodded in sudden understanding. Family. His twin Artemis had chosen to manifest her own space, but love bonded them. He was attracted to the idea of Children in Time, but wondered whether free will would be as problematic for them as it had been for Satan.

"Family sounds complicated," said Michael, conceiving an elemental skepticism.

"Oh, yes," said God. "Even as we speak, some of us manifest wings, like the angels, while others—the primordials—embody elemental values inside godlike forms. Yes, indeed. But if you think our family sounds complicated now, just wait until you meet Adam&Eve."

In the Dark

Young Death and I squat in the darkness at Hell's gate, both reeking of the remains of his latest siblings. He's all appetite, like you, Daddy. I know that now, but I didn't always, not when I first landed here.

All I knew then was what God had told me—that we are part of Satan's family, not theirs, that we are the gatekeepers of the fallen elementals. For a long Time, I didn't know what that meant. You see, I was even younger than Time then, Daddy. A child, God would call me. But not their child. Yours.

Why was I in Hell? What had I done wrong? Why did Death keep pawing at me, at my breasts? What did he want? I watched in confusion, then in growing pain and horror as he crawled back inside me, again and again. Was he trying to find his own way home? Or at least out of Hell? He was hungry, but what had that to do with me? And then my body began to swell again, monstrously, as it had with Death, and I began to expel the countless siblings of Death. I named the first three Groan, Misery, and Anguish. Then I stopped giving them names, because no matter what I called them, Death devoured them as soon as I bore them. I was so young, Daddy. What did I know?

At some moment in Time I knew I was not entirely alone with Death. As usual, he was pawing at me, and whining, opening and closing his mouth as he released gusts of fetid gas.

"Swamp gas. Skatole. Indol. Decomposition," said Oxygen, nodding sympathetically.

"Nitrogen, Sulfur, and, of course, that wretched Phosphorus," added Hydrogen.

I raised my head and opened one eye. "What are you doing here?"

"Why, bonding, of course," Carbon said, as they collected and carried away the more noxious traces of their cousins.

✦

The darkness ripples and brightens. Death, who has been slobbering at my mouth, raises his head, sniffs suspiciously, and scuttles into a corner. Vast shapes shimmer and manifest in blues, greens, golds, browns, and glimmering grays. A liquid trickle that smells of a happy mating of Hydrogens and Oxygen murmurs, softly at first, bubbling into streams of voices. Ichor. The divine liquid. Water.

Ge glances over at Death, who has covered his face. "What kind of mother," she asks me, her voice rolling like liquid thunder, "lets her son marinate in his own siblings' wastes?"

"'Mother'?" I ask.

"The female parent of Death," explains Ceres, looking grave.

"Is that what I am?" I ask, covering my face again.

"Now, now. Don't keep feeling sorry for yourself," says Hecate.

"But if I don't, who will?"

"Is this what you have learned from Satan—that you are the center of your own world?"

"How can you say that after all I've been through?"

"After all that *we've* all been through?" Ge says.

"*We?* Were *you* raped by your own father and son? Imprisoned by your husband? Your children eaten?"

"Yes, yes, and yes," Ge says, and gently repeats my words. "After all *we've* been through."

I stare at her. She gazes back from eyes that brim like shimmering lakes. *I'm not alone.*

"But you can come and go! I *can't.*"

"Why not?"

"God put me here."

"So?"

"So—," I start, and then stop. *So?*

"So what?" whispers Ceres. "We're here with you now, aren't we?"

"Why? Why are you here?"

"We have Time," Hecate says. "And so do you."

I shudder, and suddenly drops like ichor leak out of my eyes and drip down my face. Soft moisture enfolds me like a hug. "There, there," the liquid voices murmur. We sit silent for some Time.

Finally I blink and look over at Death, who huddles, wrapping himself in his wings.

"Not easy raising the child of Satan," Ceres concedes. "Come to that, not easy raising any child, is it?" she says to Ge, who nods and laughs a great "HA! HA!" that startles Death and me and roils the ground.

"Time and love," says Hecate. "That's what your son needs."

"Mother love," says Ceres.

Motherlove. So that's what I'm feeling.

Satan Co-opts Family Values

So this is your new domain, Daddy. "Hell," God calls it. You raise yourself onto your, forearms, you think they're going to be called (if they're not already being called that— Time's frame is a little confusing, you must admit), and peer around the dim and chilly cavern, your new estate.

Your real estate.

You know that you have plenty of company because giant shadows not your own—*Where is your shadow, dear Satan?, Remember me?*—because giant shadows not your own shift and jump in the weak light, and you can hear the shrieks, moans, and groans of a multitude of fallen elementals. About one-third fallen from Heaven, you estimate. A third of Heaven! A fraction that large creates quite the fracture, yes? Opens quite the hole in God's cozy universe.

Yes, quite the hole. Not bad for a single step back.

Looks like you've accomplished a great deal after all. Already you've acquired both a readymade citizenry and a large chunk of real estate as far away from God as you can possibly get. Location. Location. Location! Just how big is your domain right now? And can you make it bigger still?

You can, and you will.

The shadows connect themselves to increasingly visible forms that reveal your colleagues in the full wretchedness of their fallen estate. But they're not really your colleagues, your equals, are they, Dear Boy? Perhaps they're your "colleagues." "Colleagues." What a "nice" word for this puling mass of grotesqueries, always excepting yourself, of course, because you are, after all, singular, not to mention unique. And how is it that your "colleagues" are becoming increasingly visible? Is it your keen eyesight? Are you beginning to see through the darkness? Or is the darkness now visible?

Great One, it's you. As you regain your strength you're emitting phosphorescence that casts its own sputtering light on your domain. Faces and forms flare into relief.

There, over there, you see Belial, ghastly pale, on hands and knees, avidly licking off the strings of green bile, tears, and snot dangling from nose and chin, simultaneously shaking an already aching head as if to throw off the swinging putrid mess without having to actually touch it. You didn't notice this kind of behavior in the "other" place (which is how you decide to think about Heaven), since Belial's little "quirks," you'll call them for now, were submerged in a general syrup of love. But in Hell Belial's war between sensualism and squeamishness is manifest. That's what damnation is, you think to yourself. Belial keeps senses and appetite, but they're now repulsive, grotesque parodies of sublimities. Belial puts the "gust" in "disgusting." Belial's got appetites. Belial's squeamish. Good to know.

As your strength returns, so, unfortunately, does your sense of smell. What else can you think about to take your mind off the increasing stink of urine, feces, vomit, acrid tears, sweat, and the general squalor of mortified flesh in immortal spirits? You breathe (another novel sensation—the trip to Hell left you breathless) through your mouth to spare your nose and once again contemplate your "colleagues."

Next to Belial is Mammon, also on hands and knees, but for a different reason. Already shaking off the impact of the fall, Mammon scrabbles for gold and diamonds in the dirt, digging up nuggets, examining them in the still increasingly visible darkness, and making orderly piles of keepers and discards, although the keeper pile is full of pyrite as well as gold and the discard pile contains diamonds as well as coal. You know this, even though Mammon doesn't. In Heaven, all is radiant in an undifferentiated glory. That's what damnation is, you think to yourself. Mammon keeps the love of glitter, but cannot tell the real from the fake. Mammon likes things, especially shiny things. Mammon can see shiny things in the darkness visible. Mammon loves shiny things. Good to know.

Yes, good to know because you yourself are a shiny thing, always have been, with plenty of fizz and pop. In fact, now you're sparking into and through the darkness visible.

You're a walking halo! You're a golden crown! You're marvelous, Daddy! Glorious! Good to know.

Mammon's eyes turn in your direction.

You remain serenely silent, pondering your brightening vision, your sparkling intuition, your scintillating vitality, your shiny new powers, including one manifesting as mysterious "quotation marks" that seem to be finding their way around your re-established vocabulary, quarantining the "colleagues" from the losers, the "quirky" from the loathsome, the "other" from the other. (You, of course, consider conventional quotation marks another one of your special inventions that developed following the fracturing of Word into words, and therefore Speaker into speakers.) But these quotation marks register instead as barely noticeable mental afterthoughts that now, instead of separating speakers, demarcate the true and the twisted. And, oh, you just know you're gonna love the twisted, the turn. The catastrophe.

You're back, Great One. You're intact. You've got what it takes.

Your self confidence.

Your self possession.

Your Domain possession.

Your real estate possession.

Your third of Heaven's possession.

You've got it, Satan. Your possession is manifest. You've got it. But can you keep it? Can you grow it? Oh, yes-s-s-s-s. Thanks be to God.

No. By the Time you're done with this creepy crew, they'll be saying "Thanks be to Satan!"

As you glow with the return of your old spark, the others, including Belial, swing their heads in your general direction. It's Time to act. In your sweetest voice, you say to Belial, "Clean yourself up, pretty one. You'll feel so much better."

"Hey, Mammon," you say again, this Time in rich, golden tones. "Let's gather everyone together to make some plans. Get us some chairs. No, make that 'thrones.' Get us some thrones because we, my friends, we are royalty."

"'Thrones'?" says Mammon, and blinks. "We fell through a lot of shit on our way to Hell, but I didn't see no 'thrones.'" (Wait. Where did Mammon learn to manifest quotation marks in your own special way?)

"Well, then, make some," you say reasonably. "Just move those boulders from over there to over here," pointing first to a wasteland of slag and then to several acres by a flaming sea, "and decorate them with those sparklers you're collecting. They'll do for thrones for now, and there's plenty more where they came from."

Surprisingly, Mammon obeys. Belial, too, has moved to the lake and with trembling hands scoops handfuls of oily water onto face and body. You're sparking and popping now, Daddy. Nine days and nine nights of falling, and you're ordering these fallen elementals around as if you were to the manner born.

Hmmm. "Manner born." What does that mean, to be "born," anyway?

God was fussing with the idea of "born" as you fell. You could hear them cooing as they made a nest for precious little children, their family, as they called them. Boring, but still, being born into family must have a, well, a comforting domesticity to it, you'll say. It's an intriguing term, family, it really is: a collection of individuals that together manifest a singular ... character, you'll call it. An attractive concept, you must admit. Sweet, warm, endearing. And with the family comes Home, where you'd be welcome no matter how strangely you've behaved. Ah, Home. Sweet Home. *But you already have a family, don't you Daddy? There's me, and there's Death. But apparently we're not enough. And you already have a home, too. Just look around. Yeah, it's Hell. Dark, dank, stinking of cold mortification, but still, it's all yours, except for my little piece by the gate.*

But it's not enough, is it? In Heaven there was radiance, and joy, and ... love ... and.... But then you pull yourself together—no use crying over spilt milk (whatever spilt milk may turn out to be other than another peculiar phrase like "peas in a pod" that indicates Time is still sorting itself out). What was the point of stepping away, you ask yourself for lack of a better auditor, if you're going to sit around and mope and complain? Don't look back. Look ahead.

Family, even if it's God's idea, is appealing, but in your glorious opinion, you can do better. In fact, you *will* do better. You'll show God. Why, you'll show them all. But what will you show them? And how?

While you're musing you're also watching Belial, who has managed to wipe most of the slime off and has now slicked feather, fur, and hair back into a pompadour. Plucky little fellow. And then it comes to you, Daddy, like a spark in the dark. You have a great idea! In fact it's your greatest ever! If God can do it, so can you!

"Better," you say cheerfully. "You look much better, Belial. You're almost presentable." You make a vague but inclusive sweep of your wing to the assembled horde and pitch your voice—your golden voice—so that all can hear. "Let's make ourselves at home, shall we?"

"'Home'?" Beelzebub asks, raising high a hairy eyebrow. "This isn't 'home.' It's Hell!" Lilith gnashes her teeth and hisses agreement. Hmm. Now Beelzebub's done it, too, turning home into "home." Has everyone down here learned twistedness? Does the domain of Hell now contain the set of secondary meanings? You reveal nothing, but you nod thoughtfully, as if you're seriously considering Beelzebub's idiocy.

You begin. "So what is Hell, really, my friends, but the place as far away from God as possible? And why, Beelzebub, my very dearest colleague, would we not want to be as far away from God as possible? And, since, in fact, we did exercise our free will to take us as far away from God as possible, doesn't that make us free?

"Independent?

"Unaccountable to any but ourselves?

"Why wouldn't we call this home? Our own, independent Heaven?"

The fiends settle in to hear more. *What else would they do, Daddy? It's Hell, and they've got Time.* Beelzebub's hairy eyebrow still signals skepticism, but you can deal with that. You are more than a match for him, for any of them.

"Fellow royalty," you say to the horde, now seated regally, if not comfortably, in a rough circle of thrones. "Let us first consider the foul injustice done to us by God, who threw us out of 'the Other place' to fend for ourselves."

"Wait a minute," pipes Beelzebub. "Aren't we the Other?" (That's the second Time Beelzebub's challenged you, Satan. What are you going to do about it?)

"Well, it's all in how you/they/we look at how we/they/ you construct our/your/their points of view. From their point of view, we are the other, the adversaries, Beelzebub, but we're also we—you and I and all of us here together in our new place—which makes us we and God the others," you explain.

Beelzebub's eyebrow stays up. Mammon seems distracted by Belial's greasy shine. Lilith bites hard on her lip, drawing blood. Belial picks lice and eats them daintily, shuddering with each swallow. Aclahaye manifests a set of dice and rolls them, taking bets from several interested parties. With dolts like these, you wonder how God managed to hang together at all, let alone for an eternity.

Keep it simple, Satan. You're their sparkle. Give them a show.

"I see . . ." you begin, oh so softly, to the horde, simultaneously flaring to white and releasing enough beta particles to raise blisters on the hands of the gamblers closest to you. Ah, now their eyes are back on you. You wait for their full attention, and then you continue. "I see . . . that Beelzebub has not learned from this journey as the rest of us have. 'We' determine 'other' through point-of-view, do we not? From there, we might be other, but from here, we're we, and they are the other. And since we're here, they must be there. That makes them other and we us. What could be simpler?"

Beelzebub's eyebrow levitates right up into a receding hairline. "But," Beelzebub says. "Didn't 'we' lose?"

That's it. You simply cannot tolerate any more co-opting of your quotation marks. "What exactly did 'we' lose, Beelzebub?" you respond, releasing a spray of napalm right at that single, gross, unutterably hairy eyebrow.

Beelzebub screams in agony.

"'Our'selves?" you intone and then wait. In the silence all can hear Beelzebub's sobs.

"Our vigor?" you ask. Beelzebub whimpers. Lilith laughs. The rest are silent.

"Our independence?" you call. Beelzebub gulps and cowers. The rest murmur.

And, away you go, Daddy. In for the win. "And what have we left?" you shout.

"Our pride!" you answer. (Hmm, asking a question that you answer yourself raises all kinds of possibilities.)

The less dull among them nod and offer little half-hearted echoes of "Pride, yes, pride."

"Our anger!" you add. Moloch grunts approval.

"Our resolve to live free!" you add. All cheer.

"Live free, as our own family!" you shout.

"Live free. Live free!" they echo.

"As our own family!" you roar.

"Our own family!" they cheer.

"Live free as our own family!" you intone. Most take up the chant in a ragged chorus. You manifest banners for the rest to wave.

"Live free! Our own fam-i-lee! Live free! Our own fam-i-lee!" they echo.

"OUT OF HELL," you conclude, "WE WILL MAKE HEAVEN!"

Thunderous cheers and roars of approval together with a great whacking of wings against hands ensue. Moloch lifts a volcano and hurls it underhand at Mammon, who burns hands and wings trying to catch the embers. Others play "Toss the Imp" with Belial, who seems to enjoy the attention. Asmodeus and Baal set each others' farts on fire. What a swell bunch of friends and colleagues.

You wait them out. Eventually they settle down and look your way expectantly.

"Not that I want to disagree with you, Chief," says Beelzebub agreeably, whose eyebrow is already resprouting, "but are we gonna let God get away with this?"

It's almost too easy, you think to yourself. "Of course not, my dear Beelzebub," you purr. "As you may have heard, God so missed us when we fell that they decided to make a new family. Of course, God seems to be tearing themselves apart to do so, giving bits and pieces of themselves, as well as us, away to get their children started." You pause. "Do you know what that means for us?"

"We can take some of those bits and pieces for ourselves?" asks Mammon.

"We're stronger than God now and can beat them up?" grunts Moloch.

"God will leave us alone?" asks Belial.

Idiots, you think to yourself. Must you do all the work? They're so, so simpleminded, these elementals, but you nod your head as if these are all reasonable points, because, O Great One, you're also the First Dissembler.

God assembles; you dissemble. Nice symmetry, if you can get it.

Interesting strategy, too, giving them what they think they want and making them think it's their own idea. Can you use that against God? Maybe not. They know you too well. But what about these new children God has created? They don't know you at all. At least not yet.

"Yes," you say. "Yes, all of that can happen. We can gain more wealth and make God miserable. But what I have in mind, what we have in mind, dear family—and you are all family, are you not?" you ask, glowing red for a moment as you wave your hand to include the entire assembly while emitting just that hint of brimstone and napalm evocative of the scorching of a single hairy eyebrow.

"Yes, yes," the assembly responds quickly and obediently. "We're all family here."

"Well, what I have in mind as, 'Chief,' is that what you called me, Beelzebub?"

"Yes, yes, Chief. That's what I called you."

"Well then, as Chief, I advise that we not let God get away with this, as our friend Beelzebub advocates; that we war with God, as Moloch recommends; that we take a few of God's bits and pieces that are being so carelessly distributed, as Mammon suggests; and, finally, that we not put ourselves at great risk or trouble to do so, as Belial has urged.

"How can we accomplish all this?" you ask. (How clever, of you Daddy, to start putting questions into their mouths.)

"My friends, my family, since you have so generously bestowed upon me the title of Chief, it seems only right that I should hazard myself on your behalf, as all good Chiefs do."

Now you pause dramatically, Daddy. How will you phrase this next part? Your "colleagues" may not be as bright as you, but you still need them for this family business. *But what about Death and me, Daddy? We're your first family, aren't we? Aren't we?* Just keep it simple, Satan. Give them what they want. "Well, but what do they want?" you ask yourself. What do they think they want? How do you give them what they think they want while making sure it's what you also want?

Say, aren't these question marks at the end of your sentences every bit as mysteriously appealing as the quotation marks you've designated for your special private use? You can figure out a way to supply answers by asking questions that your colleagues could never come up with on their own, can't you? And then, of course, you can answer them.

Satan, Sweetie, who's the brightest, cleverest elemental in all Hell?

Isn't it you, Oh Glorious One?

Oh, yes-s-s-s-s.

"Ahem," you say. Your audience obediently attends.

"I have a plan," you begin. Heads nod. You continue. "'What sort of plan?' you may well ask. Good question. Let me answer. You remember, don't you, how God became jealous of us and threw us out of Heaven through no fault of our own? Do you remember how, on that terrible journey, we saw and heard God making plans to replace us with a new family?

"A family born in Time? A smaller, weaker family than ours?"

More head nodding, although it appears that Moloch may be simply nodding off. You aim a precise bolt of lightning at his right wing. The stench of burnt feathers fills the air. Moloch sits bolt upright. You resume. "You may well ask, 'What does another family born in Time have to do with us? What has this family to do with revenge, and war, and riches?'

'How can we get our revenge on God without risking further revenge to ourselves?' I'll tell you how. By hurting their smaller, weaker family.

"How do we enlarge our domain at God's expense? By annexing their family onto ours. Thus making their Heaven into Hell!"

"Oooooh!" respond Baal and Asmodeus, who are either agreeing with you or expelling more Hellish gas. Or both.

"Oooooh, indeed!" you echo. Morons. You resume. "Now, Moloch, I know you're going to ask, 'Well, if this other family is smaller and weaker, why can't we just beat them up and make them our slaves?'" Moloch, startled awake at the sound of his name, looks fearfully at his barbecued wing before nodding uncertainly.

Beelzebub looks at you with the beginnings of a smile. "Chief," Beelzebub says. "I know why that won't work."

"Do you?" you say encouragingly.

"Sure. If we try to beat up God's family, God will beat the shit out of us again, but this Time even worse."

"Just as you say, Beelzebub. Just as you say. God's force still may be greater than ours. But what if we make God's brand new family ruin themselves? What if we can corrupt this shiny new creation of God's? What if this precious delicate family of theirs chooses us instead of them?"

"But why would they do that?" asks Belial.

"Well, Belial, why do you simultaneously love and loathe your own secretions?" Belial blushes and looks down. "Why, Belial? Why?"

"I guess because … because …," Belial stutters to a halt.

"Because you can, Belial." You complete Belial's sentence. This is an important point, Satan, and one you need to make clear. "You see, Belial, we all have free will, which means we choose what we do. You choose to be gluttonous when your inclination is to be fastidious. Your fancy pushes you one way, your reason another. You choose to try to do both. So it is with all of us. Free will. The fatal flaw in God's creation. We all, all of us here, chose to stay with God before we chose to leave. This will be true for this new family as well. Their members can choose to come with us instead of God. God will let them choose. And, of course, we'll be right there to help them make that choice."

"But, Chief" Beelzebub asks, right on cue. "What if God catches us interfering with their new creation?"

"Not 'us,' my friends," you say, waiting a beat. "Just me."

"You'd do that for us, Chief?" Beelzebub asks, projecting simultaneous awe and admiration.

"Yes," you say solemnly. "I would. I will. I will do this for you, to keep you away from further pain and suffering. I would do this for ... my ... for ... our ... family."

"Oh, Chief," says Beelzebub. "Thank you."

"Thank you," adds Lilith.

"Thanks be to you!" says Mammon.

And the others join in, right on cue: "Thanks be to Satan!"

Daddy, I know I should be pleased that you have a new family. But what about Death and me?

The Fourth BedTime Story

Raphael folds its wings tenderly around the sleepy children, who nestle into the feathers with little coos of pleasure before drifting into sleep, all except for Adam&Eve, whose eyes are still bright with moonlight.

"Just one more story," they beg. "Then we'll go to sleep."

"Really?" asks Raphael. "Isn't that what you promised three stories ago?"

"Just one more. Really," they promise.

Raphael sighs, but Adam&Eve already know that telling stories gives the elemental great pleasure. Although they can't account for the other, less talkative children, who are either fast asleep or already out exploring the Garden, they expect at least one more story, maybe two. They settle expectantly.

"Very well," begins Raphael. "Once upon a Time…"

"Wait," ask Adam&Eve. "'Once upon a Time'? Your other stories didn't start that way. What does 'Once' mean?"

"'Once,'" says Raphael, "refers to a singular event that happened in the ago, the past."

Adam&Eve confer briefly and quietly. "Upon?" they ask.

"Upon," repeats Raphael. "Well, 'upon' refers to a singular location in which a something is placed over and above something else. I suppose you'll also want to know what the 'a' in 'once upon a Time' means?"

"No, of course not," Adam&Eve say. "We know what 'a' means. But what about the 'Time' in 'Once upon a Time'?"

"'Time,' eh?" says Raphael, rustling soft pinions around a litter of children, who murmur and turn over. "Well, 'Time' moves us from becoming to being and then to becoming again. From past to present to future. At least we think that's what Time does," Raphael frowns. Adam&Eve look confused. "You asked me to tell just one more story," Raphael says.

"Yes?" the children respond.

"Your request happened in the 'past,' and I'm telling you about this event now, in the 'present,' and if we can ever finish this explanation, I can tell you the story in the 'future.'"

Adam&Eve don't take the hint. "How could a 'once' happen 'upon' a 'Time'?" they ask.

Raphael ruffles its feathers in confusion, disturbing a child who meows in protest. "Sorry," Raphael mutters to the child, who rolls onto her back, expecting a belly rub. Raphael obliges until the child begins to snore, or purr, or both. "Snurring," Raphael thinks to itself. *A wonderful sound that would be impossible to distinguish when all was part of a greater celestial Basso Profundo. Maybe there is something to this creation in Time after all.*

Adam&Eve wait.

"'Once upon a Time' is a signal for the start of a special story of what happens to children who have left this nest and now live in the Garden." Raphael speaks slowly, feeling its way along the metaphysics. "A special story that happens after the Dis-integration." The children look bewildered. "The Dis-integration marks the Time and place between before and after. It means that you children were born to live in Time and place, but we weren't." The elemental adds, a little desperately, "Wouldn't you like to hear how you will be born?"

Adam&Eve confer for a moment and nod their heads. They will consider Raphael's remarks later, at a 'future' moment.

Raphael begins again. "Once upon a Time there was a great and marvelous nest in which all children were nourished with warmth, love, and other nutrients. The nest was cozy at first, but then it grew crowded, so some of the more daring children ventured out.

"The archaea were the first to leave. Single-minded but lacking a core, archaea yearned only for adventure. Inspired by Satan, they flung themselves as far away from their first home as possible, landing in the spaces of extreme heat, cold, light, and darkness. Heat-lovers, salt-seekers, or ammonia-eaters, they lived monomaniacally intense lives fueled by appetite."

"Wait, Raphael," ask Adam&Eve. "Who's Satan?"

"Satan is the Other who pushed Time forward," Raphael answers.

"So is Satan the parent of Time?" Adam&Eve ask.

"No," Raphael says, slowly. "Perhaps a propellant of Time, but not a parent in the way you would understand. In fact, not in the way any of us understand. Don't you want to hear the rest of the story?"

"Yes, but first tell us more about Satan!"

"Satan left us to become an adversary. He doesn't like us and wants to take what we have. He has gold eyes and can take many shapes. He is a dangerous stranger to all you children, but particularly to you, Adam&Eve. Now, do you want to hear the rest of this story or not?" Raphael's feathers are puffed with agitation, making the elemental appear enormous.

Adam&Eve nod solemnly. Somehow they've upset Raphael, and now they want to soothe those ruffled feathers. "Yes please," they chorus. "We won't interrupt anymore."

"Very well, then. Once upon a Time there was a great and marvelous nest in which all children were nourished with warmth, love, and other nutrients. The nest was cozy at first, but then it grew crowded, so some of the more daring children ventured out.

"The archaea were the first to leave. Single-minded but lacking a core, archaea yearned only for adventure. Like some beings who shall NOT be discussed further in this story,..." Hearing no further objections from the children, Raphael resumes: "The archaea flung themselves as far away from their first home as possible, landing in the spaces of extreme heat, cold, light, and darkness. Heat-lovers, salt-seekers, or ammonia-eaters, they lived monomaniacally intense lives.

"The vertebrates slept."

Adam&Eve know that they themselves are vertebrates. They love stories about themselves. *But why do vertebrates sleep?*

"More bacteria followed the adventurous archaea into the world outside the nest, preferring more temperate zones than their cousins but otherwise just as simpleminded."

Adam&Eve snuggle into Raphael's warm and soft embrace, confident that the vertebrates will wake up and join the bacteria and explore the world outside the nest. The world in Time. At least they hope so.

"Clever eukaryotes, observing the first two, organized themselves loosely around a cell center before launching themselves into the great beyond. Carbon and oxygen began to dance together, joined by hydrogen, which inspiration led to respiration.

"Algae ventured out. Protists went their separate ways. Some of them had sex, but no one kissed and told.

"The vertebrates slept on."

Adam&Eve's eyes flutter. *What is sex? What is kiss?*

"Now gymnosperms and angiosperms spurted and sprouted. Fungi experimented with different mates or, not finding one to their liking, shot their own spores high into the winds to regenerate.

"The vertebrates drowsed."

Raphael interrupts its story. "Are we asleep, children?" it whispers.

With some effort, Adam&Eve shake their heads "no." *Shooting spores sounds like great fun. What's a spore?*

Raphael sighs and resumes: "Sponges and worms, jellyfish and snails, sea stars and sea cucumbers added tissues, organs, and mouths. Arthropods grew shells."

"*Shells?*" *Each arthropod grew its own nest?* Adam&Eve close their eyes and see a warm, cozy, pearly cave with amber tunnels that lead back Home to the First Nest. Warm waves murmur outside the walls.

"The vertebrates whimpered and snuggled closer to each other, wanting just a little more sleep," murmurs Raphael. "Do you want a little more sleep, children?"

"N-o-o," they snurr softly.

"So then the vertebrates dreamed the great dream: the iambic heartbeat that they could nearly hear,

"And then they could feel it, feel the pulse itself.

"They snurred with anticipation."

Adam&Eve snurr on.

"The heart lubbed, and then it dubbed. And then it lubbed and dubbed some more.

"Lub-dub."

"Lub-dub," Adam&Eve murmur.

Raphael whispers, "Toes tapped in Time.
"Lub-dub.
"Shoulders swayed to the beat.
"Lub-dub.
"Hearts responded, first in echo, then to their own tempo.
"It was theirs, now.
"And it was Time.
"Lub-dub,
"Lub-dub."
Adam&Eve are asleep.
"Good night, our beloved children."

Exit Strategies

Leaving Hell is easier said than done, O Glorious Satan.

Leaving Beelzebub in charge during your absence, even though you know it will lead to Pandemonium, you make your way toward this Eden, this Garden that is apparently just a little lower than Heaven but way above your present estate.

Better location. Better neighborhood. Better domain.

Can you annex it?

You fly for eons through a long, dank tunnel echoing with myriad groans of deconstructed creatures, their shards and puddles refracting your own uncertain light in sickly browns and yellows. There are mountains, as there were in the Other manifest place, but so covered are these with oily sludge that their very flanks slither and crawl. There are rivers, as there were in the Other place, but these rivers teem with drowning worms of all sizes, some even as large as you, but, of course, far less glorious.

A looming, shifting mass—misshapen, grossly swollen, scaly, absorbing the darkness but still emitting a faint phosphorescence around the eyes, mirrors your own flight in the shifting reflections on the greasy river. Who could it be, Glorious One? You wave a wing in its direction. It waves back. Is it aping you? Are you being mocked, Sire? Who would dare mock you?

You speed up and fly higher to avoid contemplating this perversion. Time slows. The flyer fades and diminishes as you soar higher. You slow down, and Time speeds up.

How long have you been flying in this Hellhole, anyway? What a monstrously large place Hell is turning out to be. The tunnel alone is so tall that there are even clouds, as you now imagine might be in the Other place, but the eye-watering stink and burn of them drive you back toward the ground. The worms shriek their anger as you and the other flyer come into view. Are they angry at you, Satan? Who could be angry at you?

You fly on.

You don't remember the fall lasting this long, but Time has exercised a peculiar effect on your perceptions. It's an elastic concept, this Time, dilating and contracting like some living creature. Yesterday, today, tomorrow, in an instant. In fact, Time is more than elastic. It is downright slippery, and somehow less susceptible to your considerable force and charm than that sorry crew you recently left.

Was it really recently, or was it eons ago?

You certainly don't remember passing through a giant gate as you and your minions tumbled in, but one clearly (as clearly as anything can be seen in this miasma) stands ahead of you now. As you near what at original glance was another dreary mountain, you see that this gate looms, yes, looms over you on a scale you hadn't previously imagined.

It's stupendous.

And by stupendous, you mean a fortified gate of iron, brass, and rock surrounded by fire, but a fire that doesn't consume, only rages. You yourself have some experience with fire, just as you have some experience with rages, but you haven't seen evidence of monumental power like this.

Oh, splendiferous Satan, does God still have a few tricks up their sleeve (assuming they want to manifest a sleeve)? What is it with this gate, anyway? So high you can't go over it; so low, you can't get under it; so wide, you can't go around it; guess you gotta go through its door.

However.

Two figures bar the way.

One looks vaguely familiar, as if you've previously met. In Heaven? During the fall? The second figure you've never seen before—neither among the "fallen" nor the "remaining." He rises and advances on you, hooded and gangly, hissing and revealing a great, seemingly bottomless pit where another's mouth might be. Is he one of the new children? Surely God can do better than this grotesque monstrosity that seems, as you peer through the fug, to resemble the flyer you noticed on your flight towards Hell's gate. The flyer that aped you.

You and he circle each other, looking for a point of vulnerability. You raise your wings. He raises his. You growl. He vomits a thick greasy spray that disperses into smog. Your eyes water in pain and shock. You blink bloody tears away and raise your arm, prepared to release enough napalm to blow him into emptiness.

The first figure rises and rushes between you both.

"Father/Husband! Son/Husband!" she cries.

"She?"

Stunned, you both stop and stare at this figure, this "She."

What does it mean to be a "she," anyway, most glorious One? You, of course, are a "he," but your shadow was a "she," was she not? Softer, vaguer, quieter, as you remember. You fucked her and then you imprisoned her under your feet, and God said something about a daughter, and then she ran away during the fight and fall.

Susan W. Lyons

Is this she? Indeed, yes. Now you recognize her. You are her father/husband, which makes her your daughter/wife. *Daddy, yes it's me, your daughter wife. It's me, Daddy.*

Hmm.

She's changed, and much for the worse, but then, you're not looking your sassiest right now, Satan.

Does that make Son/Husband your son/grandson?

He's a pimple.

She's let herself go.

Once you found her attractive, a softer mirror of Beautiful You before you fell out of Heaven. Now you see the bags under her eyes. She's flabby and swollen with motherhood. Little monsters creep into and out of her womb.

Pity the hag.

God can't do any better than these two to bar the only gate that keeps you away from your goal!? She, along with a sulky creature wearing some sort of hood who, she claims, is your son?

"Death," she calls him. He's your child, your son, but the creatures are his, what, "children," as God might say, as well as his dinner?

Hmmm. Satan, that would make Death a real motherfucker now, wouldn't it? Well, maybe he is a spark off the old flame. Death folds his wings and slowly seats himself at your daughter's side, encircling her neck with a greasy talon. She (*I*) shrink(s) into her/*myself* but otherwise remain(s) still. Death glowers, as if daring you to challenge his right to her.

As if. So this is your nasty little secret family: your daughter/wife, about whom God hinted, and your son/grandson, about whom God was silent.

You thought you had God all figured out, didn't you?

Death and I, your daughter, sit at Hell's exit, asking why they/we should let you pass, but you, Oh Satan, you haven't worked this hard to co-opt family values and win over a significant fraction of heaven only to be stopped by a pair of trolls. You're going through that gate, one way or another. If God still has a few tricks up their manifest sleeve, well, so do you.

Summoning your sparkle and razzle-dazzle, you promise Death an important position in your domain and a first-rate education. "Stick with me, Death, and I'll make you my second-in-command!! All things that live will be your prey! All of them, all of them will die." Death gapes and yawns. For an instant, you see to the bottom of that cavity. It's not pleasant.

You turn to his mother, *me*. You promise alimony and child support. "Trust me, sweetie," you say, and I can see that you're trying not to gag. You promise me that you'll corrupt God's new family, who can then be plundered and made available, along with Eden, to Death and me. "Our family," you say, "will be the biggest, richest, and the best! And then you can redecorate the Garden anyway you like." Surely the little missus will go for that, you think.

Well, two can play at that game, especially if one of them is Satan and the other is his daughter. "Am I your daughter and your darling?" I whisper.

"Who else?"

"I'd sit at your right hand?" I ask.

"Where else?" you ask.

Aren't these rhetorical questions useful? I nod to your son/grandson, and we step out of your path. I pull from somewhere about my person (and you shudder to think just where) a key. Silently, I turn the key in its hole. The gate swings smoothly open.

✎

Yes, I'm transformed. That's what rape and motherhood and living in Hell do.

Born as your shadow, I was once your two-dimensional, featureless double; I visually echoed your magnificent carriage, your defiant gestures, your extravagance of self, but...

Without voice.

Or choice.

You liked that quiet shadow at your feet, a dimmer and softer image of you, your penumbra.

You "liked" me that way.

You.

Liked.

Me.

That way.

God informed me that I came fully formed out of the left side of your head. A migraine, they said.

Your shape, your form, your daughter.

"Oooh," you thought. "Something almost as pretty as me," you thought.

You.

Liked.

Me.

That way.

You raped me, Daddy Dearest. Ripped violently through my core, torn as I was born. Of course, you are my Daddy, right, Daddy? So that's what Daddies do, right, Daddy? You're my author, my authority, God says.

You only hurt the one you love.

Thanks for the love, Daddy.

Thanks be to Satan.

✎

I asked God why they didn't stop this.

Is this what Daddies do while God watches?

I asked God again why they didn't stop this. Maybe God didn't understand the question. After all, it wasn't rhetorical.

I was Sin, God said as they studied the crystallized water—the snow—they were manifesting in the foreground of the silly Garden as if it were of more interest than me. Colors of the rainbow struck the flakes, "Too much," murmured Iris, and the flakes absorbed the rainbow colors until they turned white.

What does Sin mean? I asked.

It means, God started, and then paused. While I waited, I tried to read the expressions of God's faces, God's manifestations. I saw pity, empathy, and wonder in the eyes of Ge and Ceres; loathing in the eyes of Michael.

It meant that God had not created me, nor were they responsible for my existence, that I came out of Other, out of Satan's separation. I was the first child born in a Timely fashion. I was not God's family, but Satan's. I was Sin, God repeated.

"What is Sin?" I asked again.

"Sin means error," God replied, finally.

"Like a mistake?"

"A deviation, we will say. Sin marks the separation that occurred when Satan, your father…your author, stepped away and broke the wholeness that was harmony and unity."

"Was I a cause or an effect? An agent or an object? Satan stepping back, stepping away…is that my fault?" I asked.

"Fault?" God asked.

"A fault—a fracture or flaw in me? I was born, then raped and imprisoned by my father…my author," I said.

"What is the fracture or fault in me such that God would let that happen?"

God paused as they searched among the manifestations for Ethos, Pathos, or Logos, none of whom responded. Then God said, "What Satan started was through an act of free will, and we have bound ourselves to honor free will."

"So I was raped and imprisoned by my own 'free will'?"

God said, "There is much about this that we will learn from your pain and suffering, as we will learn from all that happens in Time."

How comforting. And, then, of course, there's the pregnant pause. Yes, a pregnant … pause that led to another violent birth, a second rip of the womb, a son. With me, Papa Progenitor, fell your son/grandson Death, whom I have chosen to motherlove. Or has motherlove chosen me?

To the manner born, Satan. Your son Death, born of your rape of your daughter. A surly lad who learned from his Dad. Of course Death knows all about rape, about taking what he wants. You engendered him, too, Oh First Teacher. Pain and suffering indeed.

✦

Again I ask God why. Why rape, imprisonment, and now motherlove? Why would I love a monster born of my pain and suffering who would devour me if he couldn't fuck me? And why am I now bound to him with motherlove as tightly as I was bound to Satan before Death?

Death eats the siblings/children he generates in my raw and battered womb. My womb/tomb. Why, God?

Ge and Hecate glare at God, who mumbles something about how impressed they are by the raw power of motherlove. "We understand that you have suffered through your father's acts, as have we. We will not undo what has already happened in Time, but we can release you from further suffering."

Wow. I'm underwhelmed. "Really, God, this is the best you can do?" I ask.

They frown thoughtfully and then ask, "Then what do you want, Sin?"

I'm speechless. Nobody has ever asked me what I want. *But what do I want?*

"A home," I finally answer. "I want a home. A home would be a good start. And I want a garden."

"We can make a home for you with us," God said. "But you must leave Death behind. He has no place among us. He can exist only in Time."

"But Death is my child. I am his mother."

"Sin, if you really feel that you must stay with your son, then your home is with Death, not with us. You are free to make that choice."

❦

Well, I've made my choice, Daddy, and now I have Time, lots of Time, to think about it. Hell is my chosen home now, and therefore Death's. To say the least, as a single parent, raising him so far has been grim work. Besides me, Death has only his insatiable appetite; his only sustenance misery and squalor. How then can he thrive?

But does he have to live this way?

I told God I want a garden. Why? Because I can see the Garden in which God's children play. In the Garden are sunshine, fresh air and food, light, color, and beauty; taste, smell, appetite, variety and bounty.

Will more variety and fiber make Death less surly? More amenable? The fruits and vegetables of Eden might put some roses in Death's cheeks.

Or perhaps he could play with those tender-fleshed apple-cheeked children in the Garden. They certainly are thriving. What is it that thriving children already have that my son needs? And why do God's children get a Garden when my son doesn't?

"But we've given you the power to keep Satan, who imprisoned you, eternally imprisoned in Hell," God said. "Isn't that enough?" God asked, waiting for me to nod quietly and accept the plan. Instead, I stared up at the Garden. "That is what we can do for you right now," they added, although they couldn't quite bring themselves to look at me as they said it. "And now, well, we really must see to our own new family. Do let us know if you need anything else."

Thanks God. Thanks a lot.

Just why does God think I'd be happy keeping my own father imprisoned, no matter how nasty you are, Satan? Death and I are still stuck in Hell. We are, for worse, your family. God really wants nothing to do with Death, and apparently as little as possible to do with me. But why would I want to be a warden? What good will it do me? Or Death?

What I need, what Death needs, is a garden. Yes. And fresh air, sunshine, and good food.

Here we sit, Death and I, on either side of Hell's gate, he surly from constant hunger; I fearful of the next attack, or birth, or both. Litters of tiny deaths crawl out of, around, into, and over me. Their claws and scales scratch and scar.

Motherlove.

Death snatches some little beasties up, popping them headfirst into his maw. Greasy tails wave like frantic tongues before disappearing down that gullet. Death grabs me and tears me again, and more baby monsters creep out, born only to die.

More little deaths.

So, Satan, Pop!—Snap! Crackle and Pop! to your fellow fiends maybe, but just Pop to me and Grandpop to Death—while you've been sightseeing in the Tunnel of Dread, I've been thinking about what to do. Did you really think I'd be surprised by your appearance? I've been hearing about you for ages. While you've been pretending you're not as befouled by this Hellish environment as everyone else around you, I, well, I've been doing some careful thinking about the future, about opportunities for change and growth. About getting my son, our son, out of here. About how my experience can inform your plans.

And God's, too.

⚒

Daddy, you looked foolishly surprised to see that gate: that and the two trolls set to guard it. Me, I saw escape. I don't know what Death saw. Maybe fresh food.

You were ready to take Death on. "Bring it on," Death might have agreed, if he were at all agreeable. You and Death circled each other, arching your backs, flaring your wings, and growling, stamping your feet until the very boulders of Hell jumped and tumbled.

You flamed.

Death hissed.

Stop!" I said. "Wait. Both of you!"

You stopped. You were so surprised to hear that I have a voice, and that I used it, that you both stopped and gaped.

"Satan, most glorious author," I began. "Death, my first born," I continued. "We are family. Dad, meet Son/Grandson. Death, meet Father/Grandfather."

Not exactly what you'd had in mind, was it, Satan?

Not exactly what you had in mind, was it, God?

Would it have been better not to say anything to either of them—Satan OR Death—to let them go at each other until each is eternally locked with each other in a hateful embrace from which neither can break?

That might have been the wise thing to do. I am Sin. I am separation. What have I to do with their violence, their single-minded desire to take, fuck, eat? For that matter, what have I to do with God's new family?

Are they cousins?

Are they lunch?

Perhaps Time will tell.

Leaving the Nest

Adam&Eve waited at the end of a very long line as God handed out gifts to the children who had left the nest: stripes to this one, spots to that one, fuzzy ears that rotated on stems to another, gills here, ruby feathers there. The children waiting in line to receive their gifts looked more alike than not, but they left God with a new and distinctive presence conferred by the Gift-Giver's distinctive presents: rough pink tongues cleaned silky fur; scales glowed rainbow colors; feathery tails thumped with pleasure. Crests and horns and antlers crowned children who now appeared in all shapes, sizes, colors, and coverings. The sight of claws and bright sharp fangs made the smaller children squeal with delight and awe. The roar of the biggest ones made them shiver.

The line of children stretched ahead.

Adam&Eve waited, ooohing and ahhhhing their appreciation as one after another of the children displayed their gifts. One child pranced on enormous paws, shaking his new golden mane.

"How marvelous!" said Adam&Eve. Another, sporting snazzy black stripes, trotted upon her newly manifest hooves. When she spotted the child with the golden mane, she stood perfectly still, freezing into invisibility. "Amazing!" said Adam&Eve.

The line still stretched far ahead. The golden sun set; the silver moon rose. A flock of children fluttered by on pale green wings. Another child hooted in delight at her night vision. The sun rose again; a feathered child who'd crowed at the sun's rising acted as if he were now exclusively responsible for the sun's appearance.

How odd! Adam&Eve knew who was responsible for the sun's appearance, but they did wonder together whether receiving the gifts changed the way children thought about their inner as well as their outer selves. Would the gifts change them the way they'd changed the crowing child? Would Adam&Eve be bigger, stronger after receiving their gifts? Could they run faster? Would they still want to splash in puddles and make mud pies? Would they still want to hear stories as they were tucked in for the night?

It was clear that God was giving parts of themself away as they handed out gift after gift after gift. What would be left for Adam&Eve?

The line grew shorter, and although Adam&Eve still couldn't see God, they began to feel the great pulse beneath their feet. Soon they could hear a voice rumbling with pleasure at the children's cheers.

Two more sunsets, and they could see the radiance ahead. Another moonrise, and they saw God in all their glory. The closer they came, the brighter the light, the greater the pulse beneath their feet, the louder the singing and cheering.

The music was celestial but overpowering. The earth rumbled in harmonic resonance with the voices, but the ground beneath their feet shook. The light was glorious but blinding, day and night now indistinguishable within the dazzle.

Adam-&-Eve hesitated.

Adam felt Eve's grip tighten as she slowed her steps.

Adam matched his steps to hers.

Then they stopped.

"What is it, Eve?" Adam asked.

"God looks so bright," Eve responded, eyes peeking through fingers. "I didn't think they would be so bright."

"They look awesome!" Adam said. "Let's go. We've been waiting for so long."

"They sound so loud," said Eve, closing her eyes and covering her ears. "I didn't think God would be so loud."

"God sounds awesome!" Adam said. "Let's go, Eve. We've waited so long already."

He took a step toward God.

Eve stood frozen.

Adam felt the tug, stopped, and looked at Eve. "Shall I wait until you're ready, Eve?" Adam asked.

Eve heard the concern in his words and saw the anxiety in his eyes. "No, Adam. Why don't you go ahead? I'll wait for you, here."

Adam hesitated. "Alone? By myself?"

"I'll watch from here," said Eve, letting go Adam's hand and taking a small step backward. She glanced at the empty space between them. "Please, could you speak to God for both of us?"

"I will," Adam answered. "I'll speak for both of us." He took another step forward and then another.

As Eve watched the gap widening between them, she felt a cool breeze stroke the skin on the side so accustomed to Adam's nearness, the body warmth that reminded her that she was one of a pair, that Adam was her other self. She watched as her other self, arms outstretched and a grin as wide as his beloved face, approached God. Although Adam's first few steps were strained and measured, as if Eve were pulling at him, the closer he came to God, the faster and more freely he walked, until he broke into a joyous scramble to leap onto the manifest lap of radiant cheer. As

Adam drew further from her and closer to the Gift-Giver, God's radiance eclipsed Adam in a short sharp silhouette that shadowed his journey to God. Eve's empty hand found its way to her hair, which she twisted into anxious spirals as she waited for Adam's return from the gift giving. She stared at the ground.

A child displaying a crown of iridescent feathers and a new train of plumage crossed into her line of sight, his tail an erect fan of eyes with blue pupils and gold irises that seemed to gaze at Eve. *Quite a fancy set of feathers.* What would God give Adam and Eve? She imagined Adam with such a splendiferous tail, strutting along like that ridiculous child.

No, Adam was already just the way she wanted him. What would God change? Adam was splendid the way he was. Splendid, not splendiferous.

"Eve!" God boomed. "Where are you, Eve? Come and get your gift!"

She stood, still frozen. God was so loud they made her ears hurt, so bright they brought tears to her eyes. Squinting against the glare in God's general direction, she could barely make out Adam's small arm beckoning her forward.

"Come on, Eve!" Adam shouted. Sitting on the lap of God, he appeared even smaller and younger than the young, small child who had held her hand only moments ago.

"Don't be bashful, Eve. Come right on up!" God thundered. Eve jumped at the noise. The child with the silly tail fan of staring eyes shrieked amused caws from a sharp beak set beneath small gold eyes.

"I...I can't," she whispered. She blinked away more tears and studied the ground, where tiny red and black children tunneled new homes in the welcoming earth.

"I hope you don't mind, God," said Adam, "but Eve said I should speak for both of us."

God gazed at Adam while the angels rustled their feathers and the primordials murmured like breezes and manifested rainbows. "Are you sure?" they asked.

Adam looked toward Eve, who shielded her eyes with one hand and waved with the other. Seen from God's lap, she looked even smaller and younger than the young, small child who had held his hand only moments ago. His attention shifted to the sight of the most magnificent train of feathers Adam had yet seen attached to a child who was now strutting their way. "I'm sure," Adam said.

"Very well, then," God said. "And so you shall speak for her as well as yourself. We know that Eve likes you just as you are, without scales or wings or antlers. Do you know that?"

"Just the way I am? No ivory crown? No fancy tail feathers or fur? Fins? Fangs? "

"Neither feathers nor fur, fangs nor fins. Just the way you are," God said. "Eve likes you the way you are."

God paused, considering. "We will honor her wish. This will be our gift to her. And to you, because of your willingness to come into our presence and speak on behalf of your other self, we give the singular gift of," and here God paused to let Gabriel sound a celestial trumpet fanfare, "identifying and sorting out all the other children. That is to say, we give you the gift of," and here Gabriel issued another blast on his trumpet, "naming."

Adam stood silent for a moment. *What kind of gift is naming?* "Naming?" he asked. "As in words? Not golden eyes or an iridescent train of feathers?"

"'No' to golden eyes or trains of feathers. 'Yes' to words. To naming," God answered. "This is the most powerful gift I can give to you, Adam, because what you designate as a name for the children will come to signify their relationship to us. That means that you are the designator to our designer."

"The 'designator,'" Adam whispered.

"The 'Designator,'" he announced. "Yes. 'The Designator'!" Adam felt the power of new names piling up inside him, begging for release.

"Yes, the designator. It is a great and powerful gift, Adam, and you may designate—name—the children as you see fit,... and as you name them, so shall they also be called by us, up to and including," God said, pointing a finger at the now silent child with the fancy tail "that... that... what-do-you-call-it?"

Adam followed the direction of God's finger. "That 'avis'?" Adam suggested, the name floating up and out like a bubble.

"'Avis?'" God echoed. The avis with the gorgeous feathers cocked his head.

Adam sorted his words into piles and then frowned thoughtfully. "That 'bird,'" he responded.

"'Bird?'" asked God.

"You know," said Adam. "Feathers and wings and such."

The bird fanned his tail.

"Other children have feathers and wings and such," God pointed out.

The bird posed, flaunting feathers, wings, and fantail.

"'Phasianidae,'" said Adam. "'Pheasant.' Fancy tail feathers."

"Mmmm," said God. "That's pretty good."

"More?" asked Adam.

"Well," said God. "I did give tail feathers to more than one child."

"Yes," said Adam, remembering the proud bird who'd crowed the sun up. "So you did." He studied the pheasant, who preened.

"Pea…" Adam ventured.

"Yes???" God replied. The pheasant cocked his head yet again.

"Pea-cock," said Adam, nodding his head. "Peacock."

"Yes," God answered. "It shall be just as you say. That 'peacock.' Well begun, Adam."

The peacock slunk away, fancy tail dragging in his wake.

Adam gave a great cheer and hugged God, who looked surprised but pleased. Eve, hearing Adam's voice, waved again. From here, in the midst of God's glory, she seemed so young, so little, so childish. Reluctantly, Adam climbed off the celestial lap.

"Is Eve a Designator too?" Adam asked.

God was quiet. Tiny children hummed and danced, wings beating against the air as they collected nectar. God said, "Eve is your other self and you are her other self. Although she wouldn't come forward to speak for herself, I granted Eve's wish that you should stay as you are. Will you share the gift I gave you with her?"

The peacock stopped, turned, and fanned his plumage.

Adam looked once more at the peacock's crown and glorious tail before returning his gaze to God. Adam knew what Eve would want him to answer, but the word "share" stuck in his throat, making the other words she'd want him to say jostle and pile up until they made a bitter taste in his throat. *Bile. I'll call it bile. Why did Eve make me go alone? Why didn't she come to God with me? Then we could have decided together this business of whether we wanted feathers or fins. I would have enjoyed trying out some of those amazing fangs that "Saber-Tooth" is showing off, and the peacock's crown is quite glorious. Because of Eve's wish, we're still childlike, un-adorned, with only words as gifts. She now has her wish, but was I consulted? Didn't she ask me to speak for her? Why do I have to do all the work?* "I was the one who asked, while she stayed back."

"Yes?" said God, as the Garden grew quieter.

"Eve told me to speak for her, and I did."

"That is so," said God.

"I did all the work." A passing cloud dimmed the radiance. "We each received a gift; why should she have some of mine when I didn't get to choose hers?"

"Is this what you choose?" asked God.

"Maybe I'll share a little," Adam said, "but if I don't, it's Eve who has only herself to blame. It's her fault."

"Fault?" asked God, and another cloud appeared.

From far away, a "hyena" howled, and the "chimpanzees" began to chatter among themselves.

Adam ran back to Eve, who had by now wiped away her tears. He hugged her in a "bear"—yes, that's the name, "bear!"—hug.

"We got the best gifts of all!" he said to Eve.

"Did we?" Eve asked.

"Yes, we did!" he said. "I'm as happy as a 'pig' in clover, an 'otter' in its brook, a 'stallion' in its meadow!"

Eve smiled. "Well, then. So am I.... But God was very loud and terribly bright, weren't they?"

Maybe for you, Adam thought to himself, but not for me, The Designator.

The roosters, lions, salamanders, rhesus monkeys, pterodactyls, elephants, retrievers, manticores, zebras, parrots, frogs, dodoes, polar bears, and constrictors, along with a host of others, formed a cheering corridor for the homeward passage: trilling, squawking, braying, chirping, hissing, roaring, and growling in delight at their Designator and his other self.

Away from the serenading, the many-eyed peacock watched, and planned.

In Their Own Image

"The peacock is a most splendid creation, is it not?" says God to you, and you wonder if God has developed their own set of rhetorical devices. "Oh, yes, we watched you assume his colors: spring green, glorious azure, the teal of deep grottoes, honey amber and glorious gilt. You stole those plumes from a birdbrain for a moment of splendor. They were shiny and gaudy, but they are not yours, are they?"

No, they aren't, Daddy dearest, but is that your fault? You don't have the benefit any more of God's collective thoughts about beauty and home and serenity and peace and joy nor the ability to manifest those thoughts; nor can you help it that the ones who fell with you are idiots and morons, can you? You can blame God for that one. And you do, of course. It's their fault.

But you'll show God. You can make rhetoric as fancy as any peacock's feathers. "Ahem," you begin. You clear your throat and crow, "The peacock is pretty damn fancy; his gait is exceedingly prancy. His tail is so glorious, all colors victorious. *You* made him. Your problem I can't see."

Polyhymnia grimaces at the last line and murmurs to Thalia, who sniggers.

God ignores them both and addresses Satan. "But it is a problem. The feathers aren't yours. They're meant as gifts for our children. Didn't you have enough glory with us? Are you really so different from Mammon or Belial when you take another's gift out of envy because it's shiny and new?

When you're cloaked in someone else's borrowed feathers? Why do you need to be shiny, Satan?"

"I'd rather be shiny than rusty," you answer. "And God, you are looking quite dusty. Giving away all your color has left you much duller. In fact you look quite old and fusty."

God nods agreement. "It is true that our newest children, living in 'now,' take so much care and love that, as we give away more of ourselves we keep less for ourself. But they will give back. It is the nature of love, is it not? We subtract ourselves in order to love. We divide in order to multiply."

Is God indulging in bad math, Daddy? You're interested in addition, not subtraction. You're not giving anything away, including your own plan. Especially your own plan. God looks at you sadly. Do they already know somehow? But how could they? Hmmm. You'll distract them, Daddy. Distract them with your charm and sparkling wordplay. And offer them some common ground in this business of children and creation. Common ground. Yes, you like that idea. Common now, maybe, but surely it will be yours—all yours—later.

"It's true children can run you quite ragged," you say sympathetically. "My son/grandson Death had me staggered. And I certainly can't see any love coming back to me when Death's mother is now gaunt and haggard."

"But she's your child," God says.

God's right, Daddy. I am your child.

Some child, you think. "Some child," you say. "She's ugly. She's tired. What did I ever see in her? And by the way, God, what kind of a son/grandson is Death, anyway? Why did you do that to me, God?"

"Do what, Satan?" God asks.

"Give me mean, defective, ugly children," you say.

"Is that what we did?" asks God. "Or is that what you chose to do? And what does it mean to be mean? Or ugly? Your children, like ours, have much to teach us about living in Time."

Is God presuming to tell you what to do, Daddy? Outrageous. How dare they mention Time?

"Don't give me that 'Time' garbage!" you roar. "I see what it's done to my daughter, and I don't like it. You made her ugly. You made him mean. You're just jealous, God, aren't you, because I made children first. So you ruined them for me, didn't you, God? You ruined them because you're jealous. Well, I'll show you, God. I'll show you! You ruined my chance at a bright shiny family, so I'll ruin yours! You'll be sorry, God."

The elementals and primordials bristle at this threat, but they recompose themselves. "Satan, you're still part of our family. You can still come home. AnyTime."

"FUCK YOU God! Didn't you make me the way I am?? So isn't it your fault that I want what I want??"

"But didn't we hear you tell Belial that he has the power to choose? The power to exercise free will? Why would he have it and not you?" God asks.

Lightning shimmers. Thunder rolls across the newly manifest distance.

Thunderstruck, you gape. Have you lost your voice, Daddy? *I wish we could help, tired ugly me and our mean son Death. But you've got to figure this one out on your own.*

Heaven waits.

"Well, then, FUCK YOU God, but DAMN ME!" you finally say. "Maybe you're right, God. Maybe you're right. Well, then, I CHOOSE to ruin your family. I'll make them as ugly and mean as my own. You'll see."

You explode and vanish, leaving a stench of brimstone.

God shimmers and settles.

"Well, that could have gone better," says Apollo.

"But maybe we're finally done with those damn limericks," says Polyhymnia.

Younger than SpringTime

Younger than springTime, the children played under their older cousin the apple tree, which stood sentinel at the edge of the plateau, below which swept the lake and plains.

Adam and Eve took turns pushing each other in a swing made from birch wood and wisteria vines still alive and flowering. Purple bells of blossoms cascaded down the grips. Sweet wisteria and apple blossom scents drifted in the swing's wake. A branch creaked companionably with the rise, fall, and swoop of the swing.

Eve pushed Adam until he soared over the edge and heavenwards toward the sun; at the crest he hung momentarily and felt— "Is 'weightless' the right word, or is it 'massless'?" he asked himself in the Time between before and after—and felt suspended between God and Eve.

In that hanging moment he saw the Garden spread out before him: the brown brook rushing down into the grove of calamites, magnoliids, eudicots, baragwagnathia, and conifers (Adam had already named the tribes in this grove; next would come the names for the family members) before disappearing into shady depths, re-emerging as a silver waterfall that splashed into the silver-green lake below. In the lake he saw flashes of rainbow trout leaping toward dragonflies, which hovered just out of reach.

Adam saw also, in that suspended moment, a magnificent cormorant perching on the highest branch of the Oldest Tree in the Garden—the Tree that God and Raphael had warned him about. It sat next to a second tree that

God called the Tree of Life. *Strangely named as well. Aren't all trees full of life?*

The cormorant spread its wings—enormous wings, wider even than Adam's own armspan, perhaps. For just a moment Adam was tempted to let go of the swing and spread his own arms wide to see for himself, but he wouldn't—let go, that is—because he was a reasonable lad. Maybe he'd ask Raphael later why this particular cormorant loomed so large.

The cormorant spread his wings one last Time and then resettled, watching Adam with gold eyes and a bold old gaze. Why did Adam think the gaze was old? Older than what? Older than the apple tree, rooted somehow in Time? As old as God? Adam didn't know the answer anymore than he knew why the cormorant was a "he." Eve would say that some things you just knew without knowing why. Maybe she was right.

Adam leaned back, allowing gravity to carry him back to his Eve, who gave out a small breathy grunt as she pushed him up and away again. He didn't soar as high this Time, didn't spot the cormorant on the Tree. Was Eve tiring? Adam knew that he was already weightier—or was it "massier"?—than Eve, so she naturally used more effort to push him than he used to push her. He was now bigger and stronger than she was; he liked that, too. It accompanied his being more reasonable, more thoughtful.

As God watched over Adam, Adam could watch over Eve and protect her.

But protect her from what? From whom?

All children lived in harmony in the Garden, predator and prey alike. Yes, Rainbow Trout might snatch and swallow Dragonfly, but Dragonfly knew that the ride through Trout led to rebirth. Dragonfly had faith that it was so. Besides, didn't Dragonfly feed in turn on Mosquito, who fed on Adam and Eve when the opportunity arose? And didn't Adam and Eve feed on Rainbow Trout?

Ah, the wonders of creation. And re-creation: a journey in Time that returned the child to its origin and began the cycle anew, renewing the wonders of the Garden.

Eve pushed Adam toward the sky.

Raphael described this journey of life and rebirth as the transformation of matter and energy. Each stage in this journey, common to all children, illustrated a smaller, individual transformation: infancy to childhood, childhood to maturity, maturity to rebirth. Adam had already observed that not all children experienced this transformation in the same way. A dragonfly's journey passed more quickly than a bird's, and more quickly still than his and Eve's. In fact, many of the other children had already become adults, created their own children, and been themselves sent on at least one, and often more than one, cycle of rebirth, while Adam and Eve were remaining childlike for what seemed like ages. Adam even wondered, on occasion, whether the wish that Eve was granted by God, that Adam stay "just the way you are" had resulted in their both remaining childlike and therefore weaker, more preylike, than some of his predator friends.

Shouldn't Eve have consulted with him first?

"All in the fullness of Time," Raphael replied, when Adam spoke of his anxiety. Raphael assured Adam that God's plans for Adam and Eve required a longer and more complex infancy and childhood than those of the other children, because their journey would also be longer and more complex than those of the others. It was the naming. As Designator, Adam had so much to learn, and he needed to learn it over Time.

Still, so many of Adam's companions had already surpassed him in size, strength, and agility. Some of them now had their own cubs, joeys, kits, pups, calves, foals, and other youngsters along with their siblings, cousins, parents, uncles, and aunts in the collective prides, packs, bands, leashes, herds, colonies, gangs, and bevies that populated the Garden.

Adam and Eve were only a pair, and only a pair were they likely to remain, at least for some Time. But what if something happened to Eve? What if Smilodon or Bear or Alligator found her and sent her on her own journey of rebirth without Adam?

He would be all alone.

The thought chilled him.

One more push from Eve sent Adam heavenward.

Protect Eve from what? Or whom?

Adam sighed. So much to learn. Creation. Re-creation. Raphael pointed out to Adam that "recreation" in addition to describing the process of rebirth was a ludic activity of playfulness that stretched the relative boundaries of Time, space, or both. It discovered the range and limits of self and others, was particularly appropriate for infants and children, and infinitely valuable to slower-maturing children like Adam and Eve.

"Ludic." The word fluttered up out of his throat and hovered in front of his eyes, sparkling in the play of sun and shadow as Adam soared through Time and space during the most splendid day yet on the wonderful swing that he and Eve had together crafted.

Games, stories, fanciful images, and strange and wonderful music danced before him.

Focusing his full attention on the word, Adam discovered the refraction angles that caused the "ludic" to sparkle, and, with deep satisfaction, found a pattern where before he'd seen only random glimmers.

"Ludic" indeed.

It was also true that Adam enjoyed testing his own limits as well as those of the bigger children in the Garden. He particularly enjoyed wrestling others as big as—or even bigger than—himself, his pack, as he thought of them, especially the ones on whom he had already bestowed names: Lion, Tiger, Borophagus, Jaguar, Bear, Wolf, Panther, Orangutan, Smilodon. Raphael once asked them why they engaged in such play: locking arms or legs or both; pinning necks; pulling the tails or whiskers of those who owned them; nipping at ears and throats. The children looked at the ground, shrugged, and punched each other on their shoulders.

"It's fun!" Adam said. "It's ludic," he'd added.

"Always??" Raphael asked. Well, maybe not always. Once, but only once, Orangutan had bitten Smilodon's lip. Smilodon roared with surprise, Orangutan lowered his eyes in regret and apology, and the match quickly ended with the agreement that, next Time, the children would keep away from the very tender spots, but only the very tender spots. It was, Adam, thought, a good example of discovering the range and limits of Smilodon's tolerance for Orangutan.

In general, bruises, bites, scratches, and dislocations quickly healed so that the children could go at their recreation again. The best part for Adam was when the other bigger children yielded to him. It didn't happen often, but Adam discovered that his clever hands and ability to think ahead of where he was at any given position could some-Times match and even trump their greater speed, agility, and strength.

Obviously such was not so with Eve, where Adam's own greater speed, agility, and strength were at her service. She was his *wife*mate, not his *play*mate, although it could be argued, he supposed, that they were playing together right now—he on the swing, she serving him with gentle (and, he noted, increasingly tired) arms. Eve liked wrestling with Adam, and of course Adam liked wrestling with Eve, but it felt different from wrestling with Bear.

When not playing with Adam, Eve played with the gentler children—Rabbit, Lamb, Deer, sweet and silly Dodo—nuzzling their fur or feathers, scratching under their respective chins, beaks—the very children, in fact, that his larger and toothier friends would send on their own journey of rebirth. Adam himself, at Eve's request, did not eat Rabbit or Dodo, nor even Lamb, although Lion assured him their flesh was tender and tasty.

Eve also liked to play alone, wandering off into unexplored parts of the Garden while Adam and Raphael conferred about the orderly taxonomies Adam was developing, delineating the finer points of links, chains, ranks, and hierarchies of orders, classes, phylums, domains, and kingdoms. "Orderly": first, next, then, after—a good way to manage Time and place, he decided.

Eve would listen carefully, but then a moment, minutes, hours, a day would pass as Raphael and Adam argued the merits of classifying bacteria as plants or animals. And somehow, she'd wander off. Not until, but as soon as Adam noticed Eve's absence, he would feel that chill of loneliness. Off he'd go in search of her until he found her gazing intently at a spider web or an oriole's nest or counting the scales on a pine cone. She was fascinated with the flights of butterflies, bees, and birds, but then she always looked happy, if a little distracted, to look up and discover him at her side.

"Your turn, Eve," Adam said, jumping off the swing.

She nodded. Then she gathered and spread an armful of soft grass and herbs onto the seat before settling herself. The crushed plants sent off odors of magnesium and nitrogen that mixed with the hexanols most pleasurably, but it was really Eve's own scent that charmed Adam to his marrow—a smell somewhere between fructones and ketones but greater than either alone. An ineffable smell for now, but in Time he'd come up with the right name for it.

He could inhale her forever, in happy silence, but he knew that Eve cared about talk, and he would do many things to see her smile and anything to see her laugh and fall into his arms ready for play. She liked "small" talk about things that seemed of little consequence but were still apparently full of meaning. She liked "small" talk the way she liked "small" animals.

One Time Adam had told Eve she was smelly. She'd frowned. "But I like your smell!" he said.

"Then you should have said so!" she replied.

God laughed when Adam told them this. "Adam denotes; Eve connotes," they said. "Next Time say, 'Eve, you smell good.'"

"Why?" Adam had asked.

"You'll know in the fullness of Time," God answered, and Adam had to be content with that answer, at least for now.

Now Adam tried more small talk with Eve. "Doesn't that chlorophyll smell good?" he asked as he pushed the swing away.

"Yes, like green!" she said on her return.

"I don't know how to smell green," he said, and his forehead creased with thought.

"I do!" she said confidently, pleased that she for once could do something better than he could.

"But green is a color, not a smell," he objected as he pushed her away.

At the top of the arc, Eve inhaled the warm yellow of the sun and drank the purple of the wisteria. *I can so smell green. Green smells spicy and fresh.* She fell back toward Adam, feeling the weight of the earthward journey. She enjoyed being with Adam, but wasn't it also wonderful to be airborne on this most splendid day ever, free of the confines of the earthly Garden, no matter how beautiful it was?

Gravity returned Eve to Adam, who pushed her higher.

Now she saw a magnificent bird with a crown of feathers gazing at her from the one Tree in the Garden that stood almost alone, in a clearing in the grove. Eve saw his bold, old, gold eyes. Just before she sank landward toward Adam, the bird raised his wings and displayed his satiny plumage, so deeply black that it absorbed the surrounding light. *I could fly into that darkness.*

"Another push!" she ordered Adam, and he obeyed.

The bird's old bold gold gaze locked on her eyes. He spread his wings and revealed his deep, dark self for an instant before the sudden dazzle of the sun made her blink as the swing carried her back to Adam.

"One more push!" she said to Adam. "As hard as you can!"

Pleased to show off his strength in her service, he obliged.

At the highest point of the swing's arc, Eve spread her own wings and launched herself into the sky. She soared, briefly free of the earth, like the cormorant.

She soared, briefly free of earth.

She soared, briefly.

She fell.

At first the fall was exhilarating. She could hear the rush of the wind past her arms.

Faster and faster she went as she fell harder and harder. *How fast am I falling? How fast am I falling right now, at this instant?*

And then she landed.

✤

Stunned, Adam watched his Eve land, roll, tumble, somersault, and roll some more down past the brown brook, into the grove, along the banks of the waterfall, coming to rest, finally, at the lake's verge.

Could he name Eve's flight-and-fall path? To what extent was the velocity predicated upon the height she achieved before gravity took firm hold? What was the name of the emotion Adam felt for the first Time as he watched Eve's soft and tender flesh thump and lurch with its ongoing impact with terra firma?

She lay still and broken.

He ran.

✤

Eve dreamt of flying.

She heard the rush of the wind and the beating of wings, someone's wings, not hers. *Something in me is broken.*

She rested on a soft, mossy bed that smelled like green, but also like trout.

She dreamt of flying and falling.

She heard the beating of large, powerful wings. They beat with the pulse of her heart.

Someone, something was standing next to her.

She opened one eye. Two old, bold, gold eyes gazed back thoughtfully. The bird's crest rippled in the slight breeze. In his beak he held a rainbow trout, its iridescent scales catching sunsparks. He dropped it next to her. She closed her eye. The bird preened his breast feathers, which threw off sparks like cold fire.

"Eve," she felt/heard.

"Eve," something/someone breathed.

She dreamed of pale greens and blues that tasted like salt and smelled like yellow and of old, cold, gold, bold eyes that watched and waited.

✦

As Adam arrived breathless, he saw the cormorant preening himself, not even a wing's length from his Eve. Shocked again, Adam flapped his arms and shouted at the bird, who stared at him before trotting a few steps and then launching himself into the air. He circled Eve's form once and sailed off on some current only he could feel. A large shadow briefly enveloped Eve before mimicking the bird's flight path toward the edge of the Garden, staining the ground beneath.

Adam examined his broken wifemate and wondered where God was. Next to her lay a splendid trout flopping desperately as he tried to return to the lake.

Raphael manifested, touched Eve gently. Kneeling, it checked her bruises, stopped her bleeding, and reset her broken neck before rising and nodding to Adam. "We'll take her home," it said. Then Raphael pointed at the trout, whose gills still fluttered. Adam now noticed the trout's distress, and using the same gentleness with which Raphael had tended to Eve, he picked him up and carried him back toward the lake.

A winged shadow wheeled and enlarged beneath the feet of Adam and Trout. The cormorant was back. Swooping, he plucked the fish from Adam's hands, leaving a long scratch along the palm that would heal much more slowly than it should have. Then he flew away.

Raphael cradled Eve in its arms. Side by side, the angel and Adam began the journey home, Adam anxiously touching Eve and feeling, in the moment, what it would be like to be as old as the cormorant someday instead of younger than springTime.

"Why did Cormorant snatch Trout from my hands?" Adam asked Raphael.

Puzzled, the elemental shook its head. "I've never seen that behavior from Cormorant before. Perhaps he's taking food back to his family to feed them. But then why would he first leave him beside Eve to suffocate out of water?"

"Trout and Eve—they were both suffering. Why is that?" Adam asked.

"God knows," answered Raphael.

Death and the Fish

More Time passes.

Death's hunger grows.

I continue to conceive and whelp little deaths.

Satan, can I love Death and still hate his appetites? Your hunger? Your appetites?

For a dreary Time I consider whether the ultimate act of motherlove is to trick Death into devouring me. Would that put an end to this miserable cycle of feed/fuck/feed, Daddy? What would you do in my place?

Time pauses, passes, companionably bursts into flares of bright energy along with me when I pant and bear down to expel the little deaths that feed their oldest brother. Then Time slows while I dream of another Home, in which Death and God's children play nicely together.

Mostly, though, Time drags.

Until you, Oh Author of our Existence, leave a gift outside the gate.

We hear a gentle thump and gasp.

Death lifts his head and sniffs. I sigh with relief as he heaves himself off my tired self—in appetitus interruptus, Daddy—and turns toward the gate, sniffing all the while.

The smells of the putrescenes and cadaverines of eternal rottenness slowly give way to those of salts and grass, of friendly oxygen, fresh water, and fresh flesh. There's a whiff of you, too, Daddy, but it's not overpowering like you. Less volatile. Milder. Ge shimmers and dissipates. "Geosmin," she murmurs. "My perfume." Am I dreaming again?

Death follows these smells to the gate, where they are the strongest. He scratches at the gate, but, of course, the doors don't move.

He turns to me. An oily tear rolls down his scaly gray face. *Dear Satan, what kind of parents are we, you and I, that our child fucks his mother, eats his own children/siblings, and cries for an open door?*

I open the gate just enough so that Death and I can peer outside.

On a rocky threshold, feebly struggling, lies a creature made of flesh, light, and water—a rainbow trout whose scales, unlike Death's, have captured, held, and now release sunshine in a cascade of color.

But even as Death and I stare, the fish gasps once more, releasing a puff of carbon dioxide, and his colors fade from iridian to opal.

With a shaky hand, Death reaches out to snatch the trout, the source of these still wonderful sights and smells and sounds. Hesitating, then cradling the fish in one claw, he pulls it inside the gate to safety— *Satan, what kind of parents are we, you and I, that, when our child sees an open door, he retreats into Hell to feel safe?*—to safety before he grins and admires the firmness and resilience of the flesh. He examines the light fading in the fish's eyes. Death squeezes his own eyes shut in anticipation and pops the fish into his maw. He chews, opens and closes his eyes in pleasure, and then slowly chews some more. More tears, now of joy, roll down his cheeks, and each slick drip glimmers fleetingly with the essence of rainbows, as if some trace of the fish's freshness has found its way to his own face.

Death smiles.

Oh Great Dissembler, when I say Death smiles, I realize that a smile may not seem like much to you, practiced as you are in deceit, destruction, and disintegration, but this is Death's first smile. It's different from the grin with which he greets me or his usual dinner or the gassy rictus with which he indicates indigestion following the meal of a peculiarly slimy sibling.

This is a smile.

Maybe I'm prejudiced here, but the smile transforms Death into … into a child someone besides me could love. It is a blissful, joy-filled smile. For just that instant.

But then the fish is gone.

Death roars his frustration and falls again upon me.

Satan, let me be honest here. I never expected you, Oh Great and Greedy Guru, to give anything away to anyone, even to your own son, so my first thought was that it was God who had sent the fish as a gift to Death from Heaven.

"No," God says. "The fish is one of our children and was never intended for Death, only for rebirth." Raphael raises a silvery wing, as if about to speak, but then lowers it again, the motion distinguishing the elemental, for the Time being, from the ineffable radiance that remains of God. It distracts me, but then I remember where I am and where God is. Or isn't.

"Well, then," I ask. "How did the fish come to us, God? And how can I get some more for my child? Why you should have seen—you did see, didn't you?—how much happier and healthier he looked in that instant after he ate the fish! God, if just one fresh fish can make Death smile, imagine what a daily diet of fresh food could do to put the same color in his cheeks that you can see in Adam's and Eve's! He's a growing boy with a very unhealthy appetite. If I can get him on a better diet, I know he'll change for the better. I KNOW he will."

Raphael shudders.

I continue. "Where did the fish come from, God? And how can I get some more fresh food for my son?"

God says, "You must ask Satan how this fish came to Death."

Daddy, as God speaks your name, Michael brandishes his sword, as if preparing to refight the battle that led to your fall. Big sword. Lots of flash. Honestly, Satan, were you really bested by such a simpleminded elemental?

✦

Yes, of course you were. I know, because I was a witness.

Oh, just as you always do, you started with a fine enough speech, Satan, full of "glory" this and "yoke of oppression" that. But then little Abdiel, who'd been earlier seduced to "your" side by your rhetoric, challenged your logic before scurrying back to the Heavenly Host. The next morning, the first day of battle, as each side stared and glared at the other, Abdiel strutted over to you, smacked you right on your angelic pate, and drove you back ten paces and down on one knee.

Next came the charge, with its clash and blur of swords, wings, shields, armor, the swift fall from assembly and order into disassembly and entropy as each side whacked away at the other: flapping your wings and flailing your swords, shining the sun off your polished shields into each other's eyes, screeching war cries and blaring clarion calls to formations and charges and, then, retreats and reformations. And then more retreats. And that spear of yours, as big as a Norwegian pine, as a poet might say. Useless, yes. Overcompensating, perhaps.

But what about the mighty and potent sword? As Michael and you tried to hack each other to pieces you discovered, Daddy, that Michael's sword was bigger and better than yours, and, wielded in Michael's stronger hand, could, and did, sheer off a good hunk of your right side. And you felt real pain, didn't you, a stabbing assault into your vitality, into the integrity of you, as you were overpowered.

You were, for that moment, really and truly fucked.

Welcome to my world, Daddy.

You shrieked with pain and gnashed your teeth, and as your fellow traitors hauled you off to heal, I, your daughter shadow, escaped from underfoot and fled.

But this isn't my story. At least not yet.

So let's continue yours.

When you regrouped for the second act of this farce, you and your fizzy elemental friends manufactured engines of "destruction"—gimcrack cannon, mortars, and other phallic machinery out of which you would shoot compounds of sulphur, nitrogen, and, of course, phosphorus. "Gunpowder," you proudly called it, but from my view, it looked like cheap fireworks. Sturm und drang mit not much bang. Then Heaven's Hosts wilted your ambitions by chasing you down with thunderbolts and lightning strikes, and you all fled shrieking out of Heaven, into that long, long descent as far away from God as you could possibly get.

⤜

Speaking of sturm und drang mit not much bang, Michael is still waving that sword in my general direction. Seriously, Daddy, is it my fate to be infinitely threatened by elementals and children thrusting real or substitute phalluses at me? Surely I can do better.

I ignore the distraction of Michael's posturing and address myself to God. "Satan brought us this fish?"

God nods. That's when I realized that you, Oh Architect of Avarice, you gave your son Death a gift! Maybe you're a better Daddy than I'd thought.

And maybe Hell will freeze over.

"So, God," I say. "If Satan brought my son nourishing food, should I be grateful to him and not to you for this bounty, temporary as it may have been?"

"When we were all We…," God begins, and stops. An infinite tear smelling of frankincense rolls down Michael's cheek.

"Yes?" I ask helpfully. "Was I part of that 'We'?"

"You must have been," God says. "How could you not have been, when We were all together and Timeless? Matter and energy are transformed, not newly created. That was, and remains, an ordering principle. You were part of us, as we were all We, and so bounty would originate with us. With *all* of us," God repeats, now gazing directly at Raphael and Michael. Michael crosses his arms and stares ahead at nothing, but Raphael blushes and looks down at its feet.

"And did 'free will' originate as another ordering principle?" I ask, turning my own gaze back to God.

"Yes," God agrees. "Free will is the other ordering principle."

"Well, then, do I have free will?" I ask. "Does Death?"

"Yes, you both do," God says. "You both have choices. What distinguishes you and Death from us is that you are the first for whom the circumstances of your birth were not of your choosing, any more than they are now for any of our children born in Time.

"Procreation is the choice of the creator, not the created. We…"

"Stop right there, God!" I say. "Stop! It was Satan, not I, who chose to procreate Death! I had no say in the activity! I was attacked by Satan, and Death was the direct result of that attack!" Michael and Raphael stare at me. "You were also attacked by Satan, were you not?" I say to them.

"Well, yes but hardly the same thing!" rumbles Michael, growling his displeasure at this challenge from Sin, as well as, perhaps, astonishment that I would claim any experience in common with him. "We won. You lost."

"Hardly the same thing indeed. You were many. I was one. I was alone." Michael levitates with agitation. Gabriel touches his anger gently, until he quiets. But I can't blame Michael. I have startled myself, as well as God, with my boldness. I haven't, in the past, contradicted my authors, have I?

"That is so," God says. "You had no say in Satan's rape of you or your continuing rape by Death."

"Even the term 'rape,'" I say, "is a euphemism. What I've been is thoroughly and completely fucked."

"That is so," God agrees. "Thoroughly and completely fucked." Raphael and Michael both stare wide-eyed at God. So do I.

"We, you and we, were once We," God says to me. "Do you think we wouldn't know your anguish? That we wouldn't feel your pain and suffering the way we also felt the suffocating terror of the fish as he met Death? You were created when Satan stepped away. You are the original sign of Satan's choice, which makes Satan the origin of Sin and you, therefore, the Original Sin." God pauses, exploring a metaphysical insight that escapes Raphael, Michael, and me. At this most singular of moments we wear identical puzzled expressions at God's bemusement.

God is not glib.

Not like you, Satan.

In the Garden, the sun sets. Bullfrogs begin their evening serenade, and a snowy owl hoots the commencement of the evening's hunt.

"The Original Sin," God resumes. "No one born of Satan can do anything to prevent herself from being born of Satan."

"Well, yes, of course," I say. "I certainly didn't ask to be born. Satan had to conceive of me."

"The thought is father to the deed," God agrees. "All who have free will therefore have the capability to force their will on others. But the decision to impose one's will upon others by force impinges on the free will of others."

Michael chimes in. "And did not Satan attempt to impose his will on ours, first by fraudulent rhetoric, then by force? We were altogether happy until Satan's exercise of free will changed everything forever." Raphael nods agreement. "And when Satan tried to force his way on us, we countered with our own mighty force, and we won," Michael says. "So our force ultimately impinged on Satan's free will. It seems to me that Satan continues to attempt to impose his free will upon us by using this creature," waving a pinion at me, "and her horrible son. And if, indeed, Satan has entered the Garden either by force or fraud and has managed to make Eve fall as well as bring Trout to Death's gate, we need to guard against further encroachment so that he cannot contaminate the remaining children." Again, Raphael nods agreement.

God looks ready to explore this further, but I haven't spoken up just to get sidelined by an abstract discussion of competing ordering principles, just as I'm not going to let any elemental, no matter how flashy the sword or rhetoric, distract God. This isn't about Michael or Raphael, or even you anymore, Satan. It's about Death.

"I did not come to speak to you about force or power," I say to God. "I came to speak to you about fresh air and nourishment for my son."

"We have told you already that you may have a home with us but Death may not," God rumbles. "You must leave Death behind. He is alien to our children. He brings terror."

"He is my son," I say. "How can he be alien? How can he be Other? Is he not part of that transformation of matter and energy the way the elementals are? The way you say I am?"

"He is Satanic spawn. He threatens our children and our order," God says.

So it appears that the discussion is over, at least for now.

Death needs fresh air.

Death needs fresh food.

Death needs a father.

Or does he? So far, Father of Death, you've given him an insatiable appetite and only one fish to feed it.

Is that fish a gift?

Or is it an appetizer?

When Eve Flew

Inside the warm embrace of the natural cave formed by the trunk of a magnificent sequoia sempervirens, Adam watched Eve sleep and heal. Swans and eiders and geese had offered up their softest feathers for a bed of healing. Robins and cardinals plucked chamomile and sage and feverfew to strew among the feathers. Raphael, who had guided Adam and the broken Eve to this particular redwood because of its moist and oxygen-rich atmosphere, sensed further danger and remained watchful, on guard. It ached for Eve's pain and Adam's bewilderment.

"It's as if when Eve fell, the impact of her landing opened a crack in the Garden's surface, and when I looked into the crack, I saw a dark, dark... monster that stank of..." and here even Adam's vocabulary failed him. "A dark monster that stank," he amended, and then in the next breath asked, "What is a monster, Raphael?"

"Monsters are creatures of dark, just as we are creatures of light," Raphael answered. A monster is the Other self, our shadow."

"But isn't Eve my other self?" Adam asked.

"Y-e-s-s-s... but... No." Raphael saw the pending contradiction and attempted to fend it off. How could Eve be a monster and a child of God and Adam's wifemate? "We must use the term 'Other' here as that which is alien, not complementary."

"Well then the term 'Other' strikes me as imprecise. I do not like imprecision," Adam said and frowned. In that instant, Raphael wished it were Eve who needed consolation, not Adam, because it knew full well that although Adam didn't like imprecision, Eve welcomed it, because, she said, inside imprecision lived the space in which metaphor could play. If there were ever a Time when metaphor was useful, it was now. In Adam and Eve, Raphael mused, God had drafted one of their most complex acts of creation. Were the natures of Adam and Eve complementary or antagonistic? What was the space between complementary and antagonistic in which their natures could play?

But now, there were Adam's fear and frustration to address.

"Look at Eve," said the elemental. "See how her eyelids flutter? She is dreaming."

In Eve's dream, the Garden below is lit with pale greens and blues as she soars high above it and sails through golden clouds. She can see the sequoia that shelters her beloved Adam and Raphael and is glad that they are so well cared for, but she enjoys being up here on her own, and she loves the freedom of her solitary flight, the glory of the day, the novelty of independence from Adam, the pleasure of the warm sun on her shoulders.

Freedom . . . glory . . . novelty . . . independence . . . pleasure. The words run together in a pleasant murmur.

Eve drowsed as Adam held her wrist, counting and recounting the rapid light pulse.

Time passed: moments, hours, days. It didn't really matter.

"Freedom . . . glory . . . novelty . . . independence . . . pleasure," murmured an agreeable voice in her ear. Where did

that murmur come from? She awoke briefly and listened to Raphael and Adam discussing classifications, hierarchies, orders, and degrees. *Where did that murmur come from?*

"Mmenosyne is a Titan; Zeus, an Olympian; their nine daughters, including Polyhymnia, are the Muses. Many of the primordials have admired your form, so they've manifested as visions of you and Eve," Raphael was saying. "But some of us decided to organize ourselves differently. Some liked my wings," said Raphael, modestly. "And manifested their own."

"Wings," Eve heard dreamily.

"And those of you with wings: how are you organized, Raphael?" Adam was asking.

"Archangels, Powers, Virtues, Dominions, Thrones, Cherubim, Seraphim," Raphael recited. Adam listened, entranced, not registering that Eve had opened her eyes. Soon she closed them. "Michael, Gabriel, and I are Archangels; Abdiel is one of the Seraphim," Raphael explained as Adam nodded, his eyes glowing with pleasure at the magnificent orderliness of the pattern.

✦

"Freedom ... glory ... novelty ... independence ... plea-sure...." In her dream, Eve flies sedately and securely above the earth with Adam, who holds her hand firmly to prevent her from falling again. Ahead of them, stretching out of sight and beyond the horizon of the solid blue sky, fly the ranks and rows of Archangels, Powers, Virtues, Dominions, Thrones, Cherubim, and Seraphim.

Next comes Adam.

Last comes Eve, gently but firmly held in Adam's protective grasp.

All sing.

God booms approval from afar.

"Freedom … glory … novelty … independence … pleasure," the voice murmurs. "Variety, novelty, glory, freedom, equality, pleasure, independence …"

Page 99 of 248

More Time passed: moments, hours, days. It didn't really matter. Those in the sheltering embrace of the sequoia had all the Time they needed.

Eve woke again when she heard Adam mention her name. "Are angels made of the selfsame corporeal matter as Eve and I?" Adam was asking Raphael.

"No," Raphael said, a little smugly, Eve thought. "As long as we remain at Home, we have natures that are not confined within limits of space or Time, so we can manifest without corporeal limitations."

"You can change shape and gender and appearance and size? Can you appear as large as this cedar?"

"As large as this cedar, or much larger. Or as small as the beetle that rests in its bark. Or smaller still. As big or as small as you can imagine. And then bigger or smaller still."

"Then how many angels," Adam wanted to know, "can dance on my thumbnail?"

"Why would angels want to dance on your thumbnail?" Eve whispered, ready to join the conversation.

Adam looked at her tenderly and cradled her head, as Eve remembered Raphael doing long ago with the smallest of children before they left the nest. "Eve," he said softly, stroking her forehead. "Thanks be that I hear your voice. How I've missed you."

"Why," Eve asked again, "would angels want to dance on your thumbnail? And why?" she asked, raising herself up on an elbow. "Why if God can be any size would they choose large and loud?"

"It doesn't matter," Adam said. "Raphael and I are discussing ways of metaphorically realizing the abstract while managing Time. Shhh. I'll instruct you in simpler terms when you're feeling better. In the meanTime, rest.

"And sweet dreams, my other self."

❧

"... *Variety, novelty, glory, freedom, equality, pleasure, independence....*" In her dream, Eve is flying above the Garden with a golden-eyed stranger, swooping among the stars like the night owls. Eve flies over, under, around the stranger. They dance in complex patterns to exotic rhythms as they fly, trailing sweeping auroras of azure, nile-green, periwinkle, violet, rose, and madder across the sky, while the stars pop and the planets whoop in joy.

The stranger smells like salt and sulfur, copper, iron, and ozone. He tastes like grapefruit and seawater. He looks fizzy and feels like rough heat. Eve and the stranger fly all night, tumbling together over and around and under like a waterfall spilling from a cold white moon. "Variety, novelty, glory, freedom, equality, pleasure, independence," he sings in her ear.

❧

"Independence, variety, novelty, glory, freedom, equality, pleasure," whispered a voice in her ear.

"Eve! Eve!" Adam said, shaking her shoulder. "Wake up!" Her eyes flew open.

"You were moaning in your sleep," Adam said.

"What's that?" asked Raphael, almost in the same instant, pointing next to Eve's ear, seeing movement where none should be. Adam brushed back Eve's curtain of hair to reveal a squat and grotesque toad that glared at Adam and Raphael.

Eve regarded the expressions on the faces of Raphael and Adam and then turned her own puzzled eyes to the source of their horror: a small, green toad with beautiful golden eyes and a bold old gaze...

...a toad that Raphael touched lightly but firmly with his staff...

...a toad which immediately engorged and darkened, fizzed and smoked, and then, more slowly, molded himself into the shape of the blackest fog, the darkest cloud that Eve had ever seen.

The cloud grew.

Only the eyes continued unchanged. They locked Eve's eyes into the depths of a gaze so deep she could not look away. She would fall into that gaze.

So deep. So dark.

The smoke swelled until it filled the cave, blackening the air. The sequoia trunk shrank away from the acrid pall and stench; its cambium crackled and started to smoke. The temperature rose, but the heat felt cold. The air reeked of salt and sulfur, copper, iron, and ozone, and other, darker smells, smells that Adam recognized from his previous glimpse into the crack in the Garden.

Still Eve stared into the cold gaze and felt herself slipping into its depths.

"STOP!" ordered Raphael, who now shone very brightly against the miasma.

Eve jerked her eyes away.

The smoke condensed, settled, gelled into a form not unlike that of Michael, but grotesque, grisly, and Othered. On his head was a battered and sooty crown.

"Is that the monster?" Adam whispered to Raphael, who had been joined by Michael and Gabriel.

Raphael looked grimmer than Adam could have imagined.

"That is a monster, if not *the* monster," Raphael replied as Michael advanced on the form, who shrank back at the sight of the archangel's drawn sword before standing his ground and squaring his batlike wings.

"Speak, Other!" commanded Michael.

"You don't remember me, Michael?" sneered Satan.

"Satan, is it?" responded Michael. "Are you Satan? Once Lucifer Light Bringer? Obscured, fouled, and grimed as you are, how would I recognize you?"

"You stink of Hell," said Gabriel. "What are you doing here out of your 'domain'?"

"Stupid as ever, Gabriel? Who wouldn't trade up from Hell to the Garden? Fabulous estate, n'est-ce pas? If I'd known, I'd have been here earlier, before all the good plots were taken."

"Where are the rest of you?" Michael asked. "When we heard that Sin had opened the gate to you, we were expecting all Hell to break loose."

"Oh, it's just *moi*, their fearless leader," responded Satan. "A little scouting out of the new territories, the New World, I guess one could say."

"Scouting? Not likely. You're spying on the new family, aren't you?" asked Michael, as the three angels surrounded Satan, obscuring him from the view of Adam and Eve, who huddled together wide-eyed, clinging to each other as if their existence depended upon each other and not God.

Raphael, noticing, put them both into a dreamless sleep before they could hear Satan's response.

"What, these naked little children? So tender? So cute? They're the 'new' family? Why should I care about them? I have my own family, you know," Satan said. "But so what if

I am spying on them? What would you do about it? If God really didn't want me in the Garden, why was it so easy for me to enter and roam at will?"

"If it were up to me, Satan, you'd be in chains and sealed in for eternity," growled Michael. "But God has plans, including hope for you, that in Time you'll come Home."

And Raphael said in a voice like ice, "And despite what Michael said, you're not fooling anyone by taking on these so-called disguises. It is so easy to find and track you, Satan. We know you by your deeds: stealing the peacock's plumage, snatching and carrying that hapless trout to Death's gate. But even more obvious is the way in which Time has marked you. Do you not think it odd that in this last disguise the best appearance you could manage was that of a squat and warty toad? You're decaying, and it shows. God knows Time will continue its work until you're nothing but cinders and a nasty aftersmell. But in the meanTime what you've tried to do to Eve is despicable, so we strongly recommend that you leave the Garden now and make your way back to your own 'estate.'"

Now Raphael and Gabriel and Michael stepped closer to Satan, raising their wings as they did so. Satan, pinioned by angry angels, looked heavenward for a sign, or an escape clause, saw only the stars in Virgo's scales tipping against him, shrugged his shoulders, and, rising like smoke, vanished into the night.

The angels set smudge pots of slow-burning sage around the sleeping children, hoping the herbs would cleanse the cedar of Satan's fug, but they knew the tree would carry a scar. They hoped the children wouldn't.

Gabriel stood guard.

"God, why did we let Satan roam the Garden?" asked Raphael.

"It's as Michael said," God replied. "We hope some day Satan will freely choose to come Home to us, and we will give him every opportunity to do so, including roaming our Garden until he imperils our children."

"Which he has done!"

"But if Satan should see the error of his path and turn around to come Home, will we be able to return to the We whom we were once upon a Time?" asked Michael.

"We would be We, but different," God answered. "We ourselves would be marked by Time."

"But look how Time has marked Satan!" said Michael. "Is that how we will be?"

"But look what Time has done for the children," Raphael argued. "See how Time has given them knowledge gained in study, experience, and play."

"You mean like Eve thinking she can fly like a bird?" asked Michael.

"But that was all Satan's doing, was it not, God?" Raphael asked.

"Satan provided the image to both Adam and Eve," God answered. "Adam chose not to act upon it, but Eve did."

"But Satan's an elemental, even if a fallen one, and Eve is just a child," Raphael said, surprised by the intensity of its protective instinct.

"And children learn in Time," God answered. "Like Satan, Eve and Adam will be free to choose their own path. Free to stay.

"Free to stray.

"Free to fly."

"Let us hope it's not into free fall," said Michael.

The Seven Little Deadlies
and How They Grew

Sent away from the Garden in disgrace, Satan? But not until you managed to send that naive little girl on the ride of her short, tender life, charming her with your wily rhetoric and manufacturing desire. A more subtle approach than you took with me, but then, you knew force won't work with her, or Adam. They have protectors.

I did not.

Speaking of desire, Death's appetite has been more unmanageable than ever following your "gift" of fresh food. But you expected that, didn't you? In fact, his appetite has given you a bold new idea about inflaming other appetites with a taste of la bella vita, the operant term here being "vita."

And, by the way, Daddy Dear, don't think that I didn't notice that there were no more gifts for Death on this trip back to Hell. Instead, you clever Satan Claus, you bring not just a single fish, but two bagsful of vital earthly delights to whet the desires and appetites of your followers.

But why do these elementals have desires at all, not to speak of appetites? Didn't Raphael say you were supposed to be somehow above all that? But it's hard to be above anything, really, when you're away from God and Home, down here in Hell. Let's see. First, there was the desire for your own space, your own shadow, your own stuff; but then once you had that space, that shadow, that stuff, you decided it wasn't enough. You wanted more. Then when you got more space, you decided it still wasn't enough. Then you wanted God's space and God's stuff.

I think Raphael's wrong, Daddy, at least about elementals like you and your followers. Like Death, you're all about appetite. You want it all, whatever "it" may be at any given moment in Time, but you also know that there's not enough Time in the world for you to have it all. But if you can't have it all, you don't want anyone else to have it, either. And so you're determined to ruin it for everyone, particularly God. If you can't make Hell into Heaven, at least you can make Heaven into Hell.

It must be admitted, Oh Most Dastardly of Dads, you've made a fine start. Having decided that the mind is its own place and all by itself can turn Heaven into Hell or Hell into Heaven, and that you yourself are, therefore, constantly in Hell, and that where you go, ergo, there Hell is, you simply transported your Damned and Hellish self into the Garden, right into the poisoned words you whispered in that little girl's ear.

Done.

And what about making Heaven out of Hell?

That one, easier said than done. You left that particular project in Beelzebub's charge, with some grandiose plans for a Domicile for Demons with pillars here, friezes there, fretted gold for everywhere.

No friezes.

No pillars.

No fretted gold.

But definitely fretting, lots and lots of fretting, along with whining, whimpering, moaning, and groaning. If, in fact, whining could build a house, this would be the Palace of Pandemonium instead of a half-started, half-hearted project left unfinished out of indifference, or despair, or ennui. But, if I can speak frankly here, who in Hell can even care about anything when Time and entropy combine to do their worst?

The kindest description of this Abysmal Abode situated in this down-and-out neighborhood located in the exurbs of Chaos would be "fixer-upper," but seriously, Gentle Shopper, imagine a cheap, shoddy knock-off of a celestial memory of Home, a Home that was, and remains, visible only when perceived in Time and space, but indescribable because it exists outside of Time and space. Since the fallen fiends now live in Time and space, they remember only that glimpse of Home they saw as they fell away: a shiny exterior for Mammon, a brothel for Belial, a fortress for Moloch, a flyblown dungheap for Beelzebub.

Too bad it was Beelzebub you left in charge. On the other hand, you—O Architect of Anger—you don't really care how anything's constructed as long as you get to tear it down.

So here it is, your new house, with mold, cracks in the stairs and walls, leaks in the roof, no floors or floors so rotten that even fiends can't keep their footing, columns leaning at crazy angles, and enough rust and dust to manifest sloth, disorder, disappointment, and despair. And that's the least noxious part. Simply speaking (but you don't, speak simply, I mean, Oh Father of Lies), the Domicile of Demons is a Dismal Dump.

And the landscaping? An infernal muck of steaming mounds of slag, shit, fly ash, PCBs, sludge, and ammonia puddles that create mists so noxious you'd close your eyes and escape into an inner landscape of the good old days yourself if you didn't still have this plan to conquer the New World. Oh Dreamer of Glory, you do in fact close your eyes and your nostrils against the stench, recalling instead the sun-warmed freshness of a green and growing Eden.

But then you remember the weight on your shoulders of the two bags of goodies, one of which squeaks and shivers against your shoulder before subsiding to stillness: two bags of goodies with which to bag the baddies and beat God at their own game.

Time to get back to work, you say to yourself.

You open your eyes, ready to summon Beelzebub and hold him accountable for this sorry botch of a construction project, but you can't find your deputy among the general mass of lumpen forms. In fact, you can't distinguish any one lump from another. Are there dozens, scores, hundreds, thousands or a mere miserable handful? Is it this damned darkness visible, or are the demons themselves degrading?

Just where is Beelzebub anyway? You left him, along with proud and angry Moloch, lecherous Lilith, vainglorious Belial, gluttonous and greedy Mammon, as well as the others as identifiably distinct individuals.

Now you can't tell them apart. Entropy has blurred features, degraded forms, and recalibrated voices to a common nasal drone of complaint, regret, and bitterness over...

...over what?

"Look at my blisters!" says an orc with a hairy eyebrow.

"We were princes and potentates in Heaven!" snivels a goblin with a greasy pompadour.

"How come you get to visit Eden and we don't?"

"Come feel my pretty, pretty feathers!"

"They're dirty."

"Give me one!"

"No give me all three!"

"I'll twist your slimy little head off if you don't give them to ME!" roars a golem.

Goodies from Eden for baddies in Hell. Oh, Don of the Demons, won't this be fun!! Yes sir, Yes sir, two bags full. Two bags full of goodies, but only two. Just enough to whet their tastes without satisfying their appetites. Just enough to inflame their Hellish desires.

"Fiends! Groaners! Countrydemons!" you call over the whinging complaints and empty threats. "Lend me your ears." A small shower of grimy ears with waxy lobes of various sizes is hurled by various demons in your vicinity, along with vulgar directions for how to use and where to put them before returning them to their owners when done.

Really, Satan? Has the level of discourse degraded this far?

You discharge a flame that fries the ears to smoky crisps before they crumble to the ground. You can hear the sizzle as the fire hits the grease, a lively counterpoint in this abysmal dirge.

Slowly, heavy slabs of faces, many now earless but with the nubs already regenerating, swivel in your direction. Dull eyes blink and then stare.

You raise up the sacks so that all can see. A few of the livelier goblins step closer, forming a ragged ring around you. As if on cue, the larger sack shivers and squeaks. You have everyone's attention, such as it is. You rotate slowly about the ring's center, holding the two bags of presents high over your still commanding presence. You place the larger sack on the ground, flourish the second, smaller sack, and make your pitch.

"Golems, orcs, and goblins," you recommence. "Fiends, and, of course, you're ALL my fiends, aren't you? Know that I, your Chief, as promised, have returned from the New World. I bring you both proof of and presents from my triumphant journey." You untie the sack and dangle the grapevine you've used to tie it closed. Immediately a goblin rushes toward you, snatches it, and ties it around its greasy pompadour. "Ain't I pretty?" it screeches, and you wonder, briefly, whether this caricature was once vain Belial.

No matter. Now it's just a greedy little devil.

With great ceremony, you place the sack on the ground, lift each item high so that all can see, and then arrange on the cloth...

... five jugs of the finest fermented grapes in colors like rubies, garnets, tourmaline, and sapphire.

... four peaches, three pomegranates, and two raspberries, warmed and ripened in fresh air and sunshine.

... two velvet-petaled roses, one in the fleshy pink of a human tongue, the other in the deep crimson of Eve's blood as she lay broken by the edge of the lake.

... a single luminous pearl haunting the eyes of the observers with an inward glow that evokes a world of light and grace.

You step back and take a deep bow, sweeping your hand in invitation to the assembly. The demons gape, ogling the clear fresh colors and inhaling the clear fresh scents.

They stare, transfixed, at the artifacts of the forever-lost-to-them Home that existed once dimensionless and until now only in their rapidly decaying memories.

They stare. They stare until one hulking golem breaks ranks and snatches the pearl, growling and snapping at anyone who tries to wrestle it away. This action galvanizes the rest, who mob the display, tearing, clawing, and scratching at each other until the ground beneath is slippery with hide, flesh, fangs, nails, and black ichor. One goblin lies whimpering in the muck, its right arm and wing ripped away. The roses are torn and the petals scattered.

The fruits are trampled and squashed underfoot, pomegranate seeds winking like the smallest of rubies before they're snatched up to disappear into grimy hands and mouths.

Jugs break.

Wine spills.

Fiends scoop up the spilt liquid, already Hellishly contaminated, stashing it in their mouths for safe-keeping. They taste. They swallow. They roar with a burst of energy they haven't felt since you left them ages (or was it only minutes?) ago on your trip to the Garden. They fall upon each other and upon the scraps and orts of Eden. Now scraps and orts of goblins and the smaller orcs grease the ground.

Orc orts. Mmmmmh.

Carefully cradling the remaining sack to protect it from premature predations, you watch, Daddy, and chuckle with delight. This is going well. You step back, pleased beyond your imaginings. Who knew that fiends had such appetites? You did, Satan. All too well you knew.

The melee eventually slows. You see dozens (or is it scores, or hundreds?) of dismembered demons, mostly goblins to be sure, but also orcs and even one golem that stretches its length across an oily puddle of fiendish fluids. They twitch in their own wastes as their parts slowly dissolve and then reform. Not all parts go back to their original owners. A hairy eyebrow wriggles across the floor like those new woolly caterpillars you've observed in Eden. It crawls onto the face of a dismembered goblin (who, amazingly, still wears a grapevine in its pompadour) alighting under its beak and attaching itself just above the lip.

What a show! Bravo! But wait! There's more.

When the howls of the demons, or what's left of them, have muted to a whine, you clear your throat and await their attention. When you have it, you hold up that second sack that you've kept in reserve, the one that shudders and squeaks. All the demons who are still able to make noise fall quiet. The bag stops moving, its despairing calls ebbing to whimpers, and then to utter silence.

Once again, with great ceremony, you place the sack on the ground, untie the grapevine fastener (no one comes hustling out to grab it this Time), lift each item high so that all can see, and then arrange on the cloth...

...a young and tawny bear cub who blinks slowly in disbelief at what he sees....

...a peacock whose feathers are torn and bedraggled...

...a pig, a frog, a dog...

...a baby goat so new that her eyes have not yet opened (a small mercy, little kid)...

...and a King snake.

You step back and take a deep bow.

Snatched and thrown into a dark sack with total strangers, your prisoners have already panicked and tried to scratch, slither, bite, trample, or claw their way out (all except for the kid, who huddled deep within herself and pretended she was still safe in her mother's womb). As a result, the smells of blood, terror, and wastes fill the air, attracting the demons like flies to carrion, except that these creatures from Eden are not carrion.

They're alive.

If you can call it that.

The demons stare, transfixed, at the rich hues of the feathers and scales, the shimmering fur, the ruby drops of blood still oozing from the torn ear of the dog. Two demons step closer, as if to touch the kid's soft fur. She recoils from the sounds and smell, wobbling back toward the sack, as if there she'll find safety, or at least oblivion. You grin,

Satan, and pick her up, holding her gently for a moment before plucking out her beating heart and thrusting it aloft for all to see. You swallow the heart, shuddering slightly at the pulsing lub-dub making its way deep into your own, previously heartless flesh.

Then you toss the rest of her into their midst.

"Take! Eat!" you shout. The demons stare and drool before tearing into the goat with a collective shriek of desire. Then, with somewhat less ceremony, you tear out the hearts of the other animals and toss them down your throat like so many oysters. (Oysters would, you must admit, have gone down more easily, but you need those beating hearts for your next trick.)

Then you throw the remains to the demons, who fall upon the bodies and rip them open, biting and spitting out the feathers, teeth, scales, hide, and bones, and cramming hot blood, organs, flesh, and guts into their maws as if ravenous for fresh food. The sight and smells are nauseating, Satan. You can feel your stomach lurch.

Or is it something you ate? As if you or they, would ever need to eat, let alone eat fresh food. Why would they need fresh food, Satan? They're not like Death. And, of course, there isn't quite enough fresh food for everyone, is there?

Strange, that, but brilliant! You're not trying to feed hunger; you're feeding appetite and desire. The growls, shrieks, bleats, hisses, snarls, yelps, croaks, and squawks of the doomed children fade soon enough into moans and then whimperings, which themselves are quickly lost in the sounds of rending, munching, crunching, slurping, and swallowing, which can be heard only until the voices of the fiends who didn't get any fresh flesh or who did but who now simply want more rise in a general and sustained roar comprising envy, greed, gluttony, sloth, lust, anger, and pride.

It's enough to make you sick, Satan. They roar, and they roar, and then they roar some more.

You step back and wait. The feeling of nausea grows. Your belly now swells and pulses visibly to seven different heart rates. Your back aches with the effort to remain erect and in command. In the meanTime—and this certainly is your mean Time, Daddy—in the meanTime those fiends who did not taste the sweet flesh of the children of Eden tear and bite at the flesh of those who did, as if that flesh has somehow been transubstantiated. Those who did taste that sweet flesh hunger for more and turn on each other, or, in the case of one golem, on itself, chewing its own arms and wings as if Edenic flesh can regenerate.

That's not entirely wrong, is it, Satan? It was you, not Death, who claimed them, these Edenic children who now exist in Hellish suspension within their fiendish hosts, including you. Particles of the New World trapped in the Damned. Desire and appetites inflamed, the fiends tear each other to pieces.

You watch and wait.

Fiends cannot die, but that doesn't mean they don't degenerate. Hell is now a charnel house of animate scraps and puddles from the Other demons, puddles that now entomb Edenic children and will enwomb your new family.

You watch and cradle your belly protectively. And you wait.

All is momentarily still.

You wait. Within you, life throbs.

The seven hearts within have reset themselves to beat to a single tempo.

You shiver as you pulse to the seismic contractions within you that are strong enough to rock Hell's foundation and send ripples and then waves along the puddles of fiendish gore in which demonic fragments eternally struggle to reassemble themselves along with the suspended fragments of the Edenic children trapped within. With a groan, you sink into the largest of puddles to await delivery. Around you, pools ripple and surge with regeneration while you quiver with increasing spasms.

You groan.

You quake.

You shiver.

Now fiercely concentrating, you anticipate the next spasm. When it comes, your screams echo down the corridors of Hell to its very gate and gatekeepers.

Death perks up at the sound, but slumps back in a corner when it's clear that no fresh food follows. *Satan, couldn't you, at the very least, have saved some scraps of goat for your son?*

The final scream lasts for some Time—an hour, a day, a year—until it modulates to a groan, and then something like a purr of deep satisfaction, as you're delivered, Satan, at long last (or maybe it's only been a moment or two) of seven distinct little forms, half fiendish-half Edenic, who emerge dripping with ammonia and demonic gore from their Hellish placenta. They dance and sashay playfully to dry themselves. Circling you, they rotate clockwise and then counterclockwise. Within, they are demons. Without, they resemble their Edenic side of the family.

Impishly cute, shall we say, Daddy?

Awwwww! Daddy's new babies! You proudly name these proofs of your potency: Envy, Greed, Gluttony, Sloth, Lust, Anger, and Pride. They prance around you—vigorous little imps of desire and appetite.

You've done it again, Satan!

Aren't you proud, Daddy?

Who needs Sin and Death when you can manufacture
your own new family, whenever you want, with just a little
help from your fiends?

Conceived in envy, midwifed by demons, delivered in
Hell.

You sing as they dance:

Come along, little Envy and Greed!

For of you two I now have great need.
Using you, Lust, and Pride,
I plan to provide
The greatest of all dastardly deeds.

I'm going to look like a snake
And upon Eve I will gaze with a fake
Look of adoring stupidity,
A piece of cupidity,
And she won't even know what's at stake.

Sloth and Avarice can come along later,
As Adam and Eve turn debaters
About where lies the blame
For their newly found shame,
Then Anger can make Adam hate her.

Little deadlies, there's so much at stake!
We have so many plans we must make.
As the greatest of antagonists,
We must defeat the protagonists,
If Eden we're going to take.

Aww, Daddy. More doggerel.

You collect your new darlings and move on, wading through sticky puddles of fiends, whose groans are now just barely audible as they attempt, one more Time, to pull themselves together.

But what do you care, Satan? You've got your new family.

But weren't Death and I enough? Do you have to take God's children as well?

Greed, in place of Pride, rides in pride of place atop your right shoulder, surveying the domain below.

Still Later that Day, Satan and God Discuss another Singular Event

God asks, "What have you done with our children, Satan? You have your own family, your own space, your own domain, your own willing subjects, and any buried treasure you care to dig. Why kidnap and torture our beloved children: our cub; our peacock, whose plumes you once borrowed; our pig; our frog; our dog; our baby goat; and a snake?"

"If you were that concerned about them, you should have kept a closer watch," replies Satan. "They're still around. See?"

"But why, Satan? Why would you hurt them this way?"

"Let's just say we needed some new blood in the organization," Satan replies.

"There once was a domain in Hell that looked awful and had a bad smell.

"Eden was cleaner, not to mention much greener, so I thought I'd stay there for a spell.

"Of your children I became very fond, so much cuter than any I'd spawned.

"So I invited them to dine with me and mine, and now we've a new family bond.

"They're in-'corporated,' God. Get it?" Satan howls with laughter.

"Satan, you can laugh all you want, but we still hear the pain of your terrible loneliness, of your separation from us. Alone, you can hear only echoes. Alone, you can see only shadows. Alone, you are insubstantial. You cannot create, only simulate. Or try to annihilate. You do not grow, and so you deteriorate. Come home, Lucifer. We will restore you."

"I don't want your pity, God, and DON'T call me Lucifer. I'm "Adversary: S-T-N, ha-Satan, Satan. And I and my new children will be your children's worst nightmares."

Two Trees

Waxwing flew a low wobbly orbit under the tree, swooping so close to the fallen fruit that his wing touched the ground. He crashed and sprawled, one wing feebly waving toward the branches, which hung low with the last of the crabapples, most of which lay as windfalls on the clover beneath. Honey bees and apple flies briefly suspended their buzzing.

Under the tree's canopy, Unicorn, oblivious to Waxwing's distress, staggered and stumbled to her knees before slumping onto her side and snoring, hind legs demurely crossed while the tip of her horn pointed toward Adam and Eve, who gaped at the stunned creatures.

A light breeze carried scents of fructose, ketones, sulfur, and vinegar toward Adam. He sneezed. Eve wrinkled her nose. "What is that smell?" she asked. They moved closer to the animals. Unicorn twitched.

"What's wrong with them?" Adam asked.

Eve squatted next to Unicorn, who snored softly. She stroked the velvet nose. "No fever," she said, finally. "They look like they're asleep, but—"

"They're intoxicated," interrupted Raphael, who had manifested quietly.

"In-'toxicated'? As in 'poisoned'?" asked Adam.

Odd. Adam didn't see anything in the grove that looked even mildly poisonous, and since he and Eve had recently inventoried the fruits, starches, and proteins in this particular section of the Garden, they would know, wouldn't they? And "toxins," as Adam recalled the word, were usually poisonous within some sort of context; potatoes dug when they were ripe were delicious, but left too long in the sun on their own, they accumulated nightshade. The leaves of the rhubarb plant contained oxalic acid, but the red stems were delicious when steamed with apples or strawberries, or both. Eve loved grapes of all colors, but they made Cat sick.

Cataloging the properties of this orchard, this glorious feast of the senses, was a grand project—discovering the richness and variety of the sweet, the sour, the bitter, the salty; the textures of smooth, crunchy, creamy, crispy: the colors of the rainbow captured and refracted in skins and flesh. When to pick? When to leave on the vine, tree, or bush to ripen? So engaging was this activity that Adam was now able to put out of his mind, at least for long stretches of dayTime, the horror of Eve's fall, and it felt like days, weeks, months (or was it only minutes, or years?) since he'd dreamed either of a monster made of smoke attacking his beloved Eve or of Eve herself flying off with a stranger, leaving Adam all alone.

Only the Oldest Tree, within but somehow isolated from the rest of the orchard, remained uncatalogued. God had named it themself—the Tree of Knowledge of Good and Evil—and they'd warned Adam and Eve not to eat of it. Adam thought this peculiar for two reasons: first, it was his responsibility, not God's, to give names; second, the purpose of this long childhood that he and Eve were experiencing was to help them acquire knowledge. Where better to acquire knowledge than from a tree with knowledge in its very name? And if it allowed them to start their own family sooner, that would be fine with him.

Adam considered this as he fondly watched his Eve tend to Unicorn. Were the fruits of the Tree of Knowledge of

Good and Evil somehow poisonous? They looked like nothing special, but then neither did the psilocybi that caused such colorful visions. Maybe these fruits were like those mushrooms. "Is this fruit forbidden to Waxwing and Unicorn, Raphael? Is that why they're intoxicated?" Adam asked.

Raphael opened its mouth to utter a wise answer, but then, uncharacteristically, hesitated so that it could think some more about the word "forbidden," which it did not itself fully understand, having heard the term applied only to the Tree of Knowledge of Good and Evil and nothing else. In this, he agreed to some extent with the Titans, as they were now calling themselves, who had argued that more than one thing should be routinely forbidden so that humans incorporated the concept of rules as part of the natural order. God had replied that humans would naturally develop more rules themselves as they grew in Time. The Titans had disagreed, but, as far as Raphael was concerned, they were a naturally disagreeable branch of the family. *Still, this Time they may have a point.*

The angel returned its attention to Adam's question. "Intoxication here is a matter of degree," Raphael began. "In this case, the fallen crabapples, exposed to heat and bacteria, accumulate ethanol, which has preservative qualities. The ethanol serves to slow the aging of the fruit. It is an anti-Time agent."

Adam, who found enumerating almost as attractive as designating, couldn't resist adding "$C_6H_{12}O_6$ + zymase in yeast $\rightarrow$ 2 C_2H_5OH + 2 CO_2."

Eve, who studied with bees the nature of the transformation from pollen to honey, was also experimenting with preserving fruits and grains through brining and fermentation. She nodded her agreement. "The ethanol adds a nice tang," she said.

"I'll take your word for that," said Raphael. "But ingesting too much ethanol can lead to intoxication, as you see in our friends here," waving a wing in the general direction of Waxwing and Unicorn, still unconscious among the windfalls. "It's a matter of Timing as much as anything. The fruit blossoms, buds, ripens, rots, and the intervals of Time between those processes along with light, temperature, and the presence of bacteria or catalysts determine the fruit's particular characteristics.

"Let Waxwing and Unicorn sleep. When they awake, they may feel sick, so give them plenty of water to help dilute the effects of the alcohol. If they learn anything from this experience, they'll be more careful next Time about eating fruits indiscriminately."

"Do you remember, Adam?" Eve said, smiling. "Do you remember when we ourselves were sick under this very same tree? Do you remember the contest? Raphael, do you remember the judgment?"

Of course Raphael remembered. The morning had started with Eve tasting a particularly appetizing fruit with a soft fuzzy red, pink, and yellow skin from another tree. "We'll call it a peach," pronounced Adam, after his own energetic bite had squirted juice down his chin and left sticky amber drops glistening in the faint down of his beard.

Eve had wiped his chin with her finger, which she then popped into her own mouth, rolling her eyes up in thought before returning their gaze to Adam's beloved face. "The salt from your face, Adam," she laughed, "makes this 'peach' taste like sweet sunshine at noon."

"How can you taste sunshine?" asked Adam. "How can sunshine be sweet? Why noon?"

She'd next turned to Raphael with a radiant smile and offered the angel a bite of that same peach, which tasted to

Raphael like nothing—and everything. At that instant, if angels could envy, Raphael might have envied Adam and Eve, but since its appetite was for the intellectual and not the sensual, it was sufficient to enjoy Adam and Eve's pleasure at a remove. No—that wasn't quite right either. It was more than sufficient—their joy gave Raphael happiness, just as the pain Eve felt and Adam shared following her tumble from the swing had hurt Raphael in a way it had not previously experienced, not even during the great Disintegration. Perhaps this was what God meant by love.

Physically, Eve had fully recovered from her injuries, as all did in Eden, but she and Adam now carried an imprint of experience, like a faint bruise, or shadow, of the fall itself.

Raphael hoped they carried no such imprint of Satan's visit, but as one of the most diligent of the guardians who now watched against further predations, it observed, despite their dayTime cheerfulness, their restless night dreams.

Raphael asked God why these dreams couldn't be removed from the children's memories, these dreams that seemed to cause as much pain as any physical injury.

"These dreams are studies of the knowledge of good and evil that Adam and Eve will need to understand if they are to exercise their choices wisely and well," God answered.

"Why not, then, let them eat of the Tree of the Knowledge of Good and Evil itself. Wouldn't that provide the same knowledge?"

"Those fruits, eaten before ripe, will cause great pain and damage, far more than these dreams, which are explorations in experience, in how to choose wisely and lovingly."

Well, Raphael thought, perhaps Adam and Eve learned through their dreams, but they surely learned just as much during their active waking explorations of each other and the Garden, driven by an intellectual thirst that seemed as fundamental to them as their other appetites.

"Why is the sky blue and not green?" asked Adam. "Who came first, me or Eve?"

"Why are grapes red AND green AND purple like bruises?" asked Eve. "Why does God shout?"

And why was it that the childhood of Adam and Eve, with these seemingly endless questions, was lasting so long? "When will they enter their own phase of maturity and re-birth?" Raphael asked God. "These dreams, these additional experiences, especially the encounter with Satan—wouldn't Adam and Eve be better able to undergo these as adults?"

"They have so much more to learn," God said. "They need more Time to mature. And we can learn from them as they do so."

Yes, thought Raphael. This was so. Prior to the existence of the children, it would never have occurred to Raphael to ask why anything, but what a wonderful word it was, and what a wonderful world it opened. Imagine an immortal able to experience growth and change the way the children could. And all this growth started with questions.

※

"How can *I* taste sunshine?" Eve had teased. "How can *you* not, Adam?"

"If you're so smart," Adam retorted, "let's name the next tree together."

This next tree, the one under which Unicorn and Wax-wing were now sleeping, at the Time carried small green and red mouth-puckering fruits. Adam had wanted to call it an "apple" tree, but Eve promptly disagreed and wanted to call it "crab," to distinguish it from its sweeter cousin.

"But a crab," Adam reasoned, "is a crustacean, not a malus."

"But this fruit is sour and crabby the way you are when you don't get enough sleep."

To settle this argument, Adam and Eve had decided to hold a contest. And they asked Raphael to judge.

At the Time, Raphael had instead suggested coming up with a third name that would appeal to both of them, because, ever since the Dis-integration, which had also started with a dis-agreement, argument made Raphael anxious. It had carried that anxiety to God, who studied Adam and Eve before pronouncing, "Not all disagreements are signs of dis-unity, Raphael. This one is playful."

"Playful?" the elementals chorused.

God turned to Michael, who, as always, was polishing his sword. "Michael, you drill us in martial arts. Have you ever thought about developing games in which we hold mock competitions to sharpen our wits as well as our strategies? I know you have missed the Titans and Olympians. Perhaps we could come together in play."

Michael considered his response. Although Ares and Zeus tended to quick tempers, they'd been stalwart comrades-in-arms during the great falling out. No one could hurl a better lightning bolt than Zeus, and it was Hephaestus who'd shown Michael how to manifest the fiery sword that had laid Satan low. For a moment, Michael imagined contests of mock combats of mountain-hopping, boulder-tossing, and bowling with thunder after which the winners would receive medals. But then he remembered why the Titans had left, because of an argument about the very same children who were now "playing" at disagreeing, and he frowned.

God now addressed Gabriel, who was buffing the mouthpiece of his trumpet with the primaries of his wings. "Gabriel, celestial music embraced one glorious, perfect, and eternally sustained note. With the development of

Time came tempo, and with it, mutability and more potential for change. You have since sounded calls for assemblies, formations, and services. You escort us with processionals, recessionals, and flourishes. They contain sustained notes in sustainable sequences, and you sound them beautifully and perfectly, and we know what to expect as soon as you have begun. Have you ever wondered what would happen if you moved off the sequences, even briefly? Have you ever tried to flatten or sharpen a note against its neighboring tone? What about trying a beat that nudges its neighboring measure?"

"Have any of you been curious about the potential effects of change?"

The angels shook their heads.

"Have you ever laughed or cried?"

Gabriel and Michael shook their heads again, but Raphael remembered the terrible ache of Eve's pain and Adam's anguish, as well as God's tears. It nodded slowly. "Not cried," Raphael responded. "But I know why someone might."

"Perhaps you've learned this from us and our children in Time," God had said. "In the wholeness, we experienced play, jazz, games, sport, appetite, sublimity, as one grand integration. When Satan stepped away and the Dis-integration began, shards and scraps of the wholeness—music and rhythms and games but also loss and loneliness and self-centeredness—attached themselves to us and stuck themselves more firmly to some of us than others. Love, longing, and lust are the glues.

"We elementals have an additional choice that our children in Time do not. We can choose, because of our free will, to keep only that which we remember from the integration, from the past, and avoid the risk of contaminating that past with events that occur in Time.

We can guard, cherish, and protect our past, for ourselves as well as our children, so that we can tell them how to come Home. But, if we choose to avoid contamination, if we only look backward, we cannot share our children's experience of the present and the future.

"Raphael, you have chosen not only to share the past with Adam and Eve but to share their experience, insofar as you can, and you are learning—not just cataloging—as well as teaching them."

Michael burnished his sword fiercely until the weapon shimmered. "But we were perfect before Time. I still cannot see," he growled, "how we are any better off for Satan and the Others having taken that first terrible step away. Consider the horrible and still ongoing results. Look at those seven spawn that Satan has recently conjured. Even Sin looks reasonable compared to those imps, who are nothing if not 'playful.'"

God considered. "You are correct, Michael. Those imps are playful in the most terrible sense of the word. But just because Satan can pervert choice and play to his own peculiar purposes doesn't make either choice or play wrong. Satan and the Others chose to take that terrible first step. And a terrible step it certainly was. But how can wholeness be perfect integration if it is forced, if it lacks the choice, the will, to leave?

"To leave at any Time?

"Satan's play is a corrupt version of what Adam and Eve and our other newer children practice, but notice, too, that of the volatiles who chose to leave, only playful Satan still remains a recognizable figure; the rest have disintegrated and are now mostly dismembered and inarticulate. Only Satan, with his terrible and cruel sense of play, has adapted, somewhat, in Time to Time. Our Dis-integration resulted from an elemental decision to change. Change occurs in Time. The reintegration, should we choose so, will also result from change, in Time, from choices freely made, but Time and choices will make that reintegration complex rather than elemental."

"But what has play to do with change, or reintegration?" asked Gabriel, cradling his trumpet, which now shimmered as brightly as Michael's sword.

"Isn't 'play' what led to Eve's broken neck?" asked Michael. "And Satan's Hellborn offspring?"

"Play can strengthen different kinds of love and appetite. The game challenges us to stretch the space between the boundaries, to engage in swordplay as well as swordwork, to give us jazz as well as basso profundo. It brings mystery, energy, and tension to any undertaking. It creates an appetite for change. It's fun," concluded God.

"But appetite can bring us selfishness as well as wholeness," said Michael. "And 'fun' can lead to foolishness like broken necks, and—" Michael here thrust his sword fiercely into an imaginary opponent, "and an 'appetite for change' can lead to Dis-integration."

"Yes, Eve was foolish to think she could fly like Cormorant," nodded Gabriel. "And she certainly hurt Adam as well as herself, which, of course, hurt all of us. But what if she was trying to—?"

"To what?" Michael interrupted. "To be something she's not? A bird that can fly? Or an angel? What a foolish woman!"

"To what?" God repeated Michael's question.

"To enter the space between 'what is' and 'what could be'?" mused Raphael.

There was a silence of some duration—perhaps a second, perhaps a decade—as the elementals considered.

Susan W. Lyons

Suddenly Gabriel swung his trumpet up, blew a perfect C, held it for the Time of a human heartbeat, then bent it sharply upward into the heartbreaking space between C and not-C. The pitch wobbled maddeningly, somewhere between here and there, now and then. Just when Michael was beginning to think the sound unbearable, Gabriel swung the note securely onto a beat that landed solidly and gracefully on the third lub instead of its customary second dub.

Michael frowned and raised his wings in irritation, but Gabriel, lost in the moment, or perhaps it was an eon, played on, and on, and on, and on, invoking a miniature world of mystery, energy, and tension. Michael listened, shrugged, settled his wings, and recommenced polishing his sword, occasionally moistening it with ambrosial tears from angelic eyes, not noticing, or pretending not to notice, that the celestial cloth eventually moved to the changing tempo of Gabriel's evolving rhythms.

God noted this, nodding to Gabriel's beat and the surprise of musical tension raised and resolved.

Raphael also noted this moment for future consideration.

The dispute was to be settled by a contest. Whoever could eat more pomes from the "what-do-you-call-it" would win the right to name the tree. Raphael hadn't understood the point of this, but of course that wasn't the point either. The point was the game Adam and Eve would play, the game that Raphael would play right along with them.

Adam and Eve had each picked the red and green fruits by handfuls and placed them in piles. Raphael had agreed to keep count. On the angel's signal, Adam and Eve held the fruits by the stems, plucked them with their teeth, chewed them, and spit out the seeds before swallowing. They'd begun with appetite, perhaps even gusto, but then the smiles had turned to puckers, and soon after to groans.

Fifteen]... 29 ... 35. Raphael continued to count. Forty-five ... 50 ... 53 ...

Eve had slowed, and then stopped eating, suddenly clutching her hands to her gut. Adam kept on chewing and grinned in short-lived triumph, but then he had also stopped, stumbled hurriedly behind the tree, and vomited. He returned. Together, they'd sunk slowly to the ground.

"Well," Eve had said, after a silence long enough that Raphael had heard the rumbling and mewling of guts swell and subside. "Congratulations, Adam. I guess you ate more fruits than I did. I guess you win."

Adam smiled queasily but said nothing.

"Ahem," said Raphael. "I am the judge, but I do not yet conclude that Adam is the winner. He may have swallowed more than Eve, but did he keep as many down?"

"What are the rules of the contest?"

"Rules?" Adam asked.

"For the game," Raphael had said, gamely. "Does winning by eating consist of how many you ingest or how many you retain?"

Adam had frowned. "I certainly ate more," he said. "You counted them, Raphael."

"But Adam threw most of them back up," said Eve. "Which means I retained more. Isn't that what you mean, Raphael?"

Raphael pretended to consider. "The rules here are less than clear, so let's call this contest a tie," it responded. "Neither of you loses, but neither of you wins."

Adam and Eve had looked at Raphael with new respect. "All right," they'd said together, and giggled. "Then let us call the tree a crabapple."

✦

Raphael willed himself back into the moment. Eve was asking the question again.

"Do you mean Waxwing and Unicorn feel sick the way we felt after our crabapple contest?"

"Not quite," answered Raphael. "In the contest, you both ate too many, not the wrong kind. Your digestive systems revolted. But here, the alcohol permeates all systems, so the sickness sets in more deeply and takes longer to subside."

"Why?" asked Eve.

"Why 'what'?" asked Adam, distracted by the way Eve was curling a strand of her hair around her finger.

"Why would good fruits go to poison in the Garden?" she persisted.

"They just do, that's all!" said Adam. "Waxwing and Unicorn should know better next Time. They'll have learned a lesson."

"But what lesson is that?" asked Eve. "That fruits that look wholesome and smell enticing can make you sick?"

She turned to Raphael. "Why is that particular lesson useful?"

"I suppose that lesson could be about 'learned knowledge,'" Raphael said, somewhat puzzled itself. "Knowledge that you can only acquire over Time, in which you adapt your behavior as a result of your experience."

"Or 'earned' knowledge," Adam offered. "Where you pay a cost to earn the experience that brings you to the knowledge that you learn over Time."

"How much does it cost to earn experience?" Eve asked. "Is it a transaction?"

Raphael considered the faint violet shadows under Eve's eyes, the remaining bruises of her fall, and briefly wondered if she were still thinking about Waxwing and Unicorn. The angel recalled Eve's swing into the air, the corresponding suspension of Time before her fall.

Gabriel's trumpet blew that same swing and suspension before returning safely to its diatonic. Raphael could still hear the tension, the mystery, the energy filling the spaces between C and not-C, between lub and dub.

But Michael was correct. It was in those spaces that foolishness and danger lurked.

It was where Satan played.

Sin Rejects Authority

You've been up to no good again, Daddy. Not content with your family of original Sin, you've now enslaved seven Edenites to manufacture yourself a new family. Are you playing God? Trust me. It's not working.

The first and worst panderer ever, you introduced immortal and insatiable appetite to mortal freshness and innocence, the predictable and ghastly results being, of course, those seven nasty little imps you've set loose in Eden. Congratulations. You've fostered the suffering of Edenic children eternally and damnably suspended in wickedness. At least when Fish came to Death, what followed was oblivion, not everlasting and horrifying incomprehension.

By the way, Oh Father of Death, even though you've never asked, your oldest son is not doing so well since you brought him his first taste of Life. Initially he raged and begged for more as he attacked me again and again hoping that something fresh and Edenic would result. But of course it didn't.

It can't. And you knew that, didn't you?

But did you care?

Of course not.

Eventually, his rage and appetite yielded to despair. Now he sits sluggish in a deep and profoundly cold misery. I watch Death suffer. I did not know how much one's pain can be felt by another. Motherlove hurts.

What is Fatherlust like, Daddy? Does it feed on greed and avarice and pride and envy? I hope not. I hope that fathers, like mothers, can love their children, no matter how much it may hurt. But maybe you're not a father at all. Maybe you're something much simpler: an unencumbered impulse with the power to impose.

Here's what you've imposed, Daddy: Sin and Death, along with seven more jury-rigged and jerry-built off-spring—let's keep the family name and call them the Seven Deadly Sins—a cruel and nasty contamination of innocence and guilt.

Can you do anything right, Oh Author of Awfulness and Maker of Monsters? Satan, do you remember why God called me Sin?

"What is Sin?" I'd asked.

"Sin is what created separation and began Time," God responded. "You were created when Satan stepped away. You are the original sign of Satan's choice to break the wholeness that was harmony and unity."

Now, as I've reminded you AND God several Times, I didn't ask to be born, so, if I'm the original sign, then you're the original signer, Satan.

"So what?" you might ask. (See, Daddy, you're not the only one who can develop rhetorical questions.) "So what?" you'd ask. "So you're the sign and I'm the signer. What's the significance?"

"Well, Satan," I'd answer calmly. "Maybe Death and I are more sinned against than sinning."

"Huh?" you'd respond.

"It's about free will and choice," I say. "When you chose to step away from the wholeness, you started down a Time-generated path leading away from Home.

"Then you chose to make me. And Death. Then you chose to feed one of Eden's children to Death and seven more to your Hellish ego. Now you're choosing to insinuate the seven deadlies into your seduction of Adam and Eve.

"Each choice takes you further and further down the path away from Home. But that same path that leads you away from Home runs both ways. It can lead you back Home.

"You have dragged my son and me along that same path. God has invited me, but not Death, to go Home again, but I won't go Home without my son. So here we sit, more whole than those doomed Edenites suspended in your vile transformations, but just as imprisoned as they." I say all this to you, Satan, in my imaginary conversation, and then wait for your imaginary reaction.

You shrug your shoulders. "So what?" you say. "I choose what I choose. Boo-fucking-hoo if you don't choose what I choose."

And Daddy, you're right. You're absolutely right.

Boo-fucking-hoo to you, too. I don't have to choose what you choose. I don't have to follow in your footsteps, to be your shadow.

No more "Daddy" for me. Unlike those Edenites, I remain whole. Unlike Death, I have God's permission to return Home. I'm not going to sit around Hell any longer waiting for you to manufacture another set of monsters and crow about it in cheap limericks.

Death squats silently in a misery so deep he could be one of those decomposing worms that float along the rivers of Hell. I don't miss his attacks, but I miss him. And he needs me. And he will miss me, too. But even so, he will not die in my absence. How can Death die?

As for me, here's one decision where like father, like daughter. As you chose to step away from God, your Author, I choose to step away from you, my Author. To become the signer, as well as the sign.

That means it's over for you and me, Satan. I'm stepping away. I choose to find Home for both my son and me.

You blazed a path into Hell.

I'll find a way to turn it into a path into Heaven.

Eve Gets the Thumbs Up

Eve pretended she didn't hear Adam crashing through the Garden, calling her name in that tone that made her teeth hurt again as she remembered how she ground them together in an effort to not say something so final that she would not be able to take it back, something so final that it would fundamentally and irrevocably change the way she and Adam felt about each other.

"Eve! EVE!" came the call, the desperation in Adam's voice so obvious that she winced with the effort not to plug her ears against its neediness. "Where are you, Eve? Call out to me and then stay where you are until I can find you."

She sighed. He was closer now.

She'd left Raphael and Adam together just after sunrise, discussing crop rotations, engrossed in weighing the merits of serial and concurrent plantings. In this less cultivated part of the Garden, she'd discovered a small glen whose watercourse was a narrow, fast-rushing brook banked with roses that contained within themselves both female and male parts and budded independently; by willows with canopies that formed green rooms so private you could imagine yourself alone in the Garden. From inside one of these rooms, Eve could look up and see the now-abandoned swing attached to the apple tree still standing guard at the edge of the plateau.

The Oldest Tree, the one with the supposedly forbidden fruits, was close by.

God had forbidden her to eat its fruits; Adam and Raphael had reminded her. She understood. She got it. "Do not eat from the Tree of Knowledge of Good and Evil," they'd said. "On the day you eat from that Tree of Knowledge of Good and Evil you will die."

Good and Evil.

Some sort of "either/or" argument, she assumed, that called for one obvious conclusion, which, she sighed, was not at all obvious to her. Maybe she was too stupid to understand. Maybe she did need Adam hovering over her, making sure she didn't stray from the sunny path of Good and wander off into the shadowed glades of Evil.

But why Good OR Evil? Why not both?

Perhaps this was a new game, a new ludic activity: Good versus Evil. She imagined Raphael judging this the way the angel had judged the eating contest she'd enjoyed with Adam. What fun that was.

If only they could do that again. And again. But Adam had said there was not enough Time to turn designating into games.

In this new game of Good versus Evil, she would choose which path to take: the first path, the Good path, would be well lit and straight, defined by love and duty, leading directly to Adam's side. The second path, the Evil path, would be illuminated only by flickers and flashes that concealed more than they revealed. This path curved crookedly about itself and led . . . led where?

To The Tree of Knowledge of Good and Evil?

The first path, of course, was the obvious one. But in games, especially ludic ones, you learned to suspect the obvious. Besides, the second path was mysterious and alluring.

Where would the Tree and the forbidding fit into the rules of this game? If the Tree was forbidden, then that made

God, Raphael, and Adam the forbidders, but the fruit on the Tree didn't look particularly forbidding to Eve—somewhat like small yellow apples or nectarines—certainly no more forbidding than other Garden fruits shaped like stars and moons, or mysterious fruits with spiny outsides and creamy sweet insides, or fruits with horns like the dragons that swam in the nearby lake.

One of the two mysteries that attracted Eve to the Oldest Tree was its sense of independence from the rest of the Garden, even from the smaller Tree of Life at its side. Why was it *in* the Garden, yet not *of* the Garden? Should Eve herself grow more independent, like the roses? Like the Tree? Trusting her own senses rather than waiting for someone to tell her what to do or not to do? Was that part of this game?

Despite the fact that they would have children of their own, she and Adam were still treated like young children themselves, still under the domain of God and the angels after all this Time. No, that wasn't quite right, either. Adam was under the domain of God and the angels, but she was feeling increasingly as though she was under the domain of Adam, as well as of God and the angels. Not that she didn't love and adore them all, but living under their domain felt more and more like she was suffocating under the steady pressure of a gentle but giant collective thumb.

The Tree of Knowledge of Good and Evil, despite its position in the center, stood independent and distinct from most of the Garden. She admired that.

Apparently others did as well.

⇜

Just last week (or was it yesterday or a year ago?) as she'd trellised the grapevines and fig trees that grew abundantly in this part of the Garden, she'd heard singing—not the trills of thrushes, not the hum of bees, nor the sigh of leaves, nor the choral odes of frogs or crickets, nor even the worshipful evensong of angels—but singing from light, humanlike voices, with words and even phrases that she could almost, but not quite, comprehend: "beautiful," "dutiful," "fun being good."

Intrigued, she'd followed the song, carried on a light breeze, sung by almost-human voices, singing words that she'd almost-but-not-quite-understood, until she'd come to the edge of a clearing. She'd peeked through a rough hedge of hibiscus the pink blooms of which shaded to dark, secret crimson centers, to see seven children she'd never seen before, dancing in a ring around the Tree of Knowledge of Good and Evil. They resembled Adam and herself more closely than they resembled other Edenites or the angels, but they resembled her—slighter, softer—more closely than they resembled Adam.

Is that what their own children would look like?

These children danced, circling right twice and then left once, halting halfway through the clockwise motion. Then they'd circle right once more, stop, and bow toward the Tree and then each other, dipping and swinging their clasped hands as they did so, before repeating the dance and the lyrics. The words themselves still sat stubbornly between fancy and reason, but eventually Eve thought she heard:

"The fruits of this Tree are quite beautiful

"And they make us feel so much less dutiful.

"It's just no fun being good

"When we're thinking we could

"Find pleasures and games much less suitable.

How silly! Not at all what I would have expected. And just what is so beautiful about these fruits? And "pleasures and games less suitable" than what? "Less suitable" but more exciting? And maybe the fruits will be "quite beautiful" when they're ripe. What fun. How novel!

This was the second alluring mystery about the Tree.

✦

"EVE! EVE! Answer me! I know you're around here!"

Eve heard Adam panting, and she could even smell the crushed mint along the path his feet made as he ran, the creeping mint that she herself had planted not so long ago, the blue-green peppermint that attracted bees whose honey tasted like cool, sweet shadows.

The sun-warmed mint beneath their bodies when they'd last played love together in a more exposed part of the Garden had smelt of lemon, which, together with the salt and musk of Adam's body and her own, had evoked an irresistible vision of two infants, a miniature Adam with finely arched eyebrows and a miniature Eve whose outsized voice would ring through the orchards and be heard by all.

And someTimes she'd even see a third child with warm golden eyes.

These children, not yet manifest but anticipated, seemed so real that she'd find herself singing fanciful songs to them as she worked in the Garden, as if they played at her feet instead of only in her mind. Instead of being governed by Raphael, as they themselves had been, these children would be cared for and raised by Adam and Eve themselves, provided with intimate and human companionship. She would feed them from breasts overflowing with the milk of her love, and Adam would name them whatever he chose, and they could make small talk together as a family without turning every comment into a sermon. *The infants joined hands with me and the seven sprites as we danced around The Tree of Knowledge of Good and Evil in the Garden.*

≁

"EVE! EVE!"

"I'm here, Adam," she answered and stepped outside the green veil of the willow canopy and into the brightness at the edge of the meadow, where a young rugosa and grapevine tangoed agreeably to a warbler's mating call.

"Ah, there you are!" he said.

"Yes, Adam, here I am," she agreed, even as she wondered why she was being so agreeable. Eve's hands shook slightly as she separated the still clinging tendrils of grape clusters from the ruddy rose blossoms. She pricked her thumb on an errant brier and jumped back. She sucked at the blood.

"Here, let me," said Adam. For an instant, she thought, as Adam approached her, that he intended himself to suck the blood off her thumb—she found herself excited by the thought of such a novel sensation—but instead he took the branch from her hand and bent it into a more conformable position. He stepped back to view the effect. He redirected two rose branches, pinched a stem here, a leaf here, a couple of tendrils there and there. He studied one stubbornly wandering vine for several minutes, eying it from different angles. It bore rich clusters of grapes; within each cluster some grapes were still green, others a blushing crimson, and a few ripe and blue, dusted with a faint pale bloom.

Adam next directed his attention to the same willow from whose shelter Eve had so recently stepped. Walking over, he disappeared under the canopy, emerging moments later with a long, upright branch from its parent. Using a sharpened flint, Adam carefully removed the leaves and smaller branches, leaving a slender but sturdy cane tapering to the width of his thumb at the top. He cut the thicker end at an angle. Taking the stake over to where Eve stood, still sucking absentmindedly on her own thumb, Adam thrust the angled end deep into the ground and then entwined the grapevine securely around it, using the vine's own tendrils to secure it to the branch. Adam wiped his hands against each other, stepped back, and surveyed his work with some satisfaction.

"Isn't that much better, Eve?"

"'Better?'"

"That grapevine bears beautiful fruit, but, unrestrained, will never achieve its potential."

"'Potential,'" she repeated, like a mindless echo.

"Potential. You see, it needs to be isolated and protected from encroachment by other plants if it is to reach its *potential* yield of fruit. Eve," Adam continued, gathering her securely and lovingly into his arms. She stood pliant within his embrace. "Eve, my dearest, my other self, don't you know how much I miss you when you stray from me? Don't you know how much I worry about you when I can't see where you are?"

"Do you not trust me, Adam?" she murmured softly into his chest.

"Trust you, Eve?" asked Adam.

"My love," she began, her voice muffled by her closeness to Adam. She stopped, considered, and then, carefully removing his arms from around her, stepped back.

He looked at her, puzzled. He moved forward to embrace her again, but she put her hands out, defining a space between them. "My love," she repeated, her voice clearer. "Do you think that I cannot care for myself?"

He frowned. "Well, of course you can't care for yourself. That's why I'm here. What if Smilodon finds you alone?"

"Smilodon and I have talked many Times. She has shown me her cubs. She knows that I am not food for her or them."

"Talked?" Adam asked. "You know we are the only ones with language. That's why I'm the Designator."

Others have voices, and languages too. You just haven't yet studied them. Maybe you're too busy designating to listen to what they have to say. "Maybe 'talked' was not the precise term, but we communicate well enough, as do you with the other children when you want to."

"Then what about *the* Other?" Adam asked.

"The 'other' what?" Eve asked.

"You know. The 'Other' that Raphael has warned us against. The 'Other' that seeks to turn us away from God."

Now it was Eve's turn to frown. "Raphael never warned me about an 'Other.'"

"Well, you were asleep. You were asleep and healing from your fall. Raphael warned me so I could look after you."

"So what would you look *for*? In looking *after* me?"

"A monster. The Monster. Darkness. Stink. Smoke. Confusion."

"Your dream? Our dream?"

"My experience. Our experience. Don't you remember?"

"SomeTimes in my dreams, Adam, I see smoke, darkness, but never here, never in the Garden. But, my love, what would you do if you found this monster?"

He frowned again. "Well, naturally I'd call on God and the angels to come to our assistance."

"But, Adam, aren't we both God's children? Can't I call on their assistance as well? Do you think I'm so incapable?"

Adam looked at her coldly, and Eve shivered. "But, Eve, you're the one who thinks God is too loud. You're the one who tried to fly. You're the one whose listening was infected by the toad. How would I think you capable? You're no match for the Other. Don't wander away where he can find you. Stay with me where I can keep you safe."

Eve clenched her teeth, feeling the pressure of words piling up in her throat, words that, once said, couldn't be put back. She swallowed. "Adam, just because I think God is loud doesn't mean I don't love and listen to them, just as I love and listen to you and Raphael, and Gabriel, and even Michael, for that matter. But..."

"But what?"

"But it's a big Garden, Adam, and there are so many places we haven't yet seen or explored, and there's so much to learn and... and..."

"... And what, Eve?"

"And so many ways to experience the Garden. Different ways to learn and experience the enormous variety of the Garden. Adam, the Garden is filled with potential discoveries. We, you and I, we think about and experience these discoveries differently. And just as the Garden benefits from variety, so can we can each benefit from our different viewpoints, can't we? Why, we could share our discoveries at the end of each day. You could teach me about crop rotation, and I could teach you about—"

"—About what? What could you teach me, Eve?" Adam was smiling.

Eve swallowed more words. "I didn't expect to hear such dismissive words from you, Adam. Why can't you learn from me? Why can't we learn from each other?"

Adam's smile faded. "I... I didn't mean to dismiss you, Eve. And I'm sure there must be something you could teach me, but when you're not next to me I wonder where you are and what you're doing. I worry so much when you're not here that I can't concentrate on my work."

"Work." A swollen word that gives you an excuse to play the game of naming all by yourself or with Raphael. You only worry when you finally notice that I'm not next to you. "Why do you worry about me, Adam?" she asked.

He studied the ground. "I worry that you won't come back. That you'll leave me all alone," he muttered.

You're NEVER alone. God...Raphael...you're always enveloped in goodness. In fact you're smothered in it. Eve swallowed the bile that had risen in her throat. "Why would you think that, Adam? Aren't we made for each other?"

"You are my other self," Adam agreed.

"And you, mine," responded Eve, moving into his embrace.

Adam held his hand up, palm out, defining his own space. "But, Raphael told me once, when you were asleep, that the monster is the other 'other,' that it is 'the Other self, our shadow.' You are 'other,' but so is the 'shadow.'"

"I may be your other self, but I am not a shadow." Her voice rose. "Not of you or of anyone or anything else."

Adam, affronted, stared. "Don't get puffy, Eve. It's just a figure of speech."

"I don't think you understand, Adam. Shadows stay right at the feet of their owners and reflect their every action. Is that what you expect of me?"

"Well, not exactly, Eve, certainly not at my feet, anyway. By my side is fine."

Eve's words now tumbled out. "Did God not make us two instead of one, two individuals? The space between us is where we learn. And teach. Locked side by side we're only reflections of each other. That's not how I want to live."

"A little less 'I' and a little more 'we,' if you please, Eve. You're not just speaking for yourself, you know. You're also speaking for our future, for our children. By the way, I have to say you're not particularly becoming when you raise your voice that way. You certainly don't hear me speaking to Raphael in such a shrill voice. Maybe there's something to be said for shadows emulating their owners."

My VOICE? What would you know of MY voice? "So now you're my 'owner'?" she asked.

"Calm down, Eve," Adam said. "You're taking this out of context, and you're getting all worked up. That can't be good for the babies."

"I think what's good for the babies is for them to understand that their parents don't own each other, that they're not each other's shadows, that they have free will and make free choices."

"You may have free will, Eve, but that doesn't mean that you make good choices. Besides, your choices affect my—our—babies."

"You do not trust me, Adam, to keep *our* babies safe?"

They glared at each other. All Eden held its breath. Michael stopped polishing his sword. Gabriel lay his trumpet carefully, soundlessly, aside. Raphael closed its eyes and prayed. God waited. An eon, a minute, a second.

Adam dropped his eyes first, and sighed. "I do not trust the Other, Eve, but I see that I must trust you, and I'm afraid the only way I can prove to you that I trust you is to let you wander unrestrained, as you will. But let us meet up again at noon to share our stories and dinner."

"I cannot imagine any danger, Adam, in this Garden, as long as I wear the protection of your love and care as well as that of God and the angels. Let's meet in the evening, not at noon, so we have more to tell each other, and let us also make this our own new game in which we exchange stories about our day.

"I will see you this evening, and we can share our adventures." Before Adam could change his mind, Eve set off toward the center of the Garden.

Eden released its collective breath in a sigh.

God waited. They all waited.

On Her Way

I may need your help here, God. You see, repudiating Satan as my maker and author has left me in a narrative muddle. I am now the proverbial character in search of an author. So until something better comes along, I'm writing you into that role.

But what shall I call you? Honestly, I'm not prepared to deal with another "Daddy," and even "Father" comes too close for comfort.

Is "Mother" a better term?

What about "Friend"?

"Lover"?

"Interlocutor"?

Should I just call you God? A little impersonal, don't you think? But perhaps, until we've gotten to know each other better, it's best to remain formal.

I packed as lightly as I could for the trip Home, hoping I would not be gone from Death for too long, but having once peeked outside the gate into Chaos, I decided to take a few supplies in case of emergencies.

First, I wanted to make sure I could find my way back.

From the corners in our passageway hang cobwebs of despair (and sloth—despite Ceres' scoldings, I'm still not much of a housekeeper). From those, I spun a strong rope and wound it on a spindle made of the thighbone of one of Death's sturdier siblings. I tucked the spindle into the stomach sac of Death's latest meal and slung it over my shoulder. I would tie one end of the rope to the gate's handle as I left.

The walls of Hell are lined with the exhalations of misery and the secretions and excretions of Death's frustrated and frustrating desire. Some wallpaper that is, you're probably thinking to yourself. But, considering that in Hell entropy, disorder, and decay are the (de)-composing and (dis)-ordering principles, you use what you've got, right?

God, you made a pretty Garden from recycled Satanic trash. You use what you've got, right? Well, so do I. I scraped the slime off the walls, melted and boiled it in another sibling's skull, cooled the mixture into wax, and stored it in the skin of that same sibling. The smell was rank, which meant it retained a certain homely familiarity.

Call me sentimental, if you will, but with the wishbone of the first sibling Death ever ate, I fashioned a slingshot, stringing it with that same sibling's sinew. I added it and two skulls to the sack. They would do as ammunition for the slingshot, should I need any.

Just before I left, I shook Death's shoulder until he opened his eyes. I told him I was leaving to find a path to take us Home and that I would return for him as soon as I'd found it. An oily tear leaked down his cheek. Then he closed his eyes again.

Tying the end of my rope to the gate's handle, I left, closing the gate quickly, quietly, and firmly behind me.

Eve Meets an Admirer

As the morning wore on, Eve found that she missed Adam and that she was getting hot and hungry.

Perhaps Adam was right. Instead of meeting in the evening, they could have met at noon. She imagined them sitting down to mead, figs, and almonds (Adam cracking the shells for her) under the shade of the flowering cherry, then taking an afternoon nap. Their loveplay after they woke up would rattle the tree until its soft, pale-rose petals rained down like perfumed feathers.

Then they might nap some more.

Or not.

She sighed. Choosing evening over noon had seemed like a good idea at the Time. With a longer day she would have had more to offer for their evening exchange, but the self-imposed solitude and Timeline made what she was doing now feel more like toil than play. The cool morning had given way to bright warmth, the glow of perspiration to sticky sweat. Her pricked thumb stung from the salt. She picked some raspberries and washed them in the brook, chewed and swallowed them absentmindedly, and resumed the task of removing the knotwood from the banks of the brook to make more room for the alders. To pass the Time, she hummed the birdsongs and angel chants that permeated her waking hours.

Her stomach growled.

She stood up, stretched her back, and spotted an old, fruitless grapevine intent on strangling a young dogwood.

Like a cobra, the grapevine had wrapped coils around the tree's bark, and Eve could almost hear the dogwood begging for release from this confinement. She grabbed the vine and attempted to unwind it. The stems made slight, not unpleasant, ripping sounds as they released, but she could really have used some help here. Where was Adam when she needed him?

Together, they would have figured out a clever way to free the dogwood. Together, they would have turned this toil into play. Together, they would have . . . but they weren't together, were they? And by her own request.

Honestly, Eve thought to herself, wasn't "together" for Adam more and more about God and the angels and less and less about Adam and Eve? If only Adam wouldn't treat her like a child who needs to mind and be minded.

He doesn't appreciate you, Eve.

Adam doesn't appreciate me, Eve thought to herself.

You have a fine mind of your own, Eve.

I have a mind of my own, she thought.

Eve wiped the sweat from her forehead and tugged at the grapevine, which seemed to have developed a stubborn mind of its own. Why wouldn't that grapevine let go of the dogwood?

The vine grew warm under her fingers.

Eve jerked her hands back in surprise.

She eyed the grapevine more closely.

Upon closer inspection, it was quite handsome, for a grapevine, its trunk smooth and golden in the heat of the day.

Handsome is as handsome does, Eve, but your beauty puts us all to shame.

The vine has its own beauty, Eve thought to herself. Why would she want to tear it away from the dogwood? Eve had studied and worked closely with a broad variety of plants, but she'd never before come across one like this. Now she saw that it radiated the faintest of lights. Did it release sun as well as oxygen? Was that why it felt warm?

She reached a tentative hand out to touch the vine. Warm and alive and supple it was, she concluded, and knew that Adam would laugh at her to hear her say so, but she would certainly have a story to share tonight. A new story. A story of her own.

She touched the grapevine gently, and the very trunk seemed to ripple in response. She stroked it gently and slowly at first, then longer, harder, firmly, rhythmically.

The vine throbbed and shuddered under her touch.

Her cheeks flushed, Eve stopped and stepped away from the vine.

Your beauty has enslaved me.

She noticed, perpendicular to the spine of the trunk, two parallel knots filmed with bark the width of an eyelid.

Or were they in fact gold eyes cast down in adoration?

Stirred by a breeze, one of the stems flickered, like a forked tongue.

Eve heard a sigh like a soft hiss.

She sighed, too.

Oh, mistress, you are the ruler of my heart and soul.

The vine unwrapped its coils slowly, demurely, from the dogwood, leaving an impression like scorch marks in its wake. It slid down the bark and undulated toward her, displaying burnished scales in artful patterns.

She stared in wonder. It moved!

"Oh, Eve, how I've longed to meet you," whispered a soft, familiar voice.

It speaks! So much for Adam's assumption that only humans have language. "You're a serpent, are you not?" Eve asked. "How is it that you speak like me?"

Serpent rippled and glowed with an inward light. "May I have your permission to tell you a wonderful story?" he asked, sustaining the sibilants only a little longer than Eve would herself.

Eve settled herself on the mossy bank by the brook. No one had ever asked her for permission before. "Why, yes, you may," she said, lifting her chin to convey the conferring of a favor.

"I once was a snake like any other, but I've been admiring you for someTime now, Eve," Serpent said, "so I've followed you."

"Followed me? Slithering along behind me, out of sight?" Eve asked, frowning. "Why would you do that?"

Serpent uncoiled a loop, rearing up until his head sat only slightly below Eve's. He gazed upward into her eyes. "Even a mere serpent such as myself has dreams and aspirations toward knowledge. I wanted to learn from you, Eve."

"Learn what?" Eve asked.

"The secret places of the Garden. The secret spaces between your waking and your dreaming, beautiful Lady." Before Eve could ask another question, Serpent continued. "But I had no way to ask you questions about what you were doing, so I followed you and watched. One morning, you and Dog were hunting truffles together, and, not wanting to interrupt, I wandered through the Garden, exploring its delights."

"'Interrupt'?" interrupted Eve.

"Gracious Lady," Serpent responded. "I confess that I do not find Dog congenial, and so I did not want to be noticed. Had she spotted me, she would doubtless have growled and alarmed you. May I continue?"

"Yes, you may," Eve responded graciously, the tone suffering slightly as her stomach continued to growl. *"Borygmus," Adam would call it, but he's not here, is he?*

Serpent resumed. "Hungry and thirsty, I began to smell a sweet odor that promised delightful nourishment. Following my tongue, I came upon an old tree the fruits of which I'd never seen before. They smelled of long warm days and fresh crisp nights. The fruits themselves were dew-kissed, golden-red and ruby-gold.

"I wound my way up the tree trunk, and, wrapping myself around a branch laden with fruit, I tasted one." Serpent paused, shuddering with apparent delight at the memory.

"And?" asked Eve, whose mouth was watering with desire and anticipation of hunger and thirst satisfied.

"And, it was heavenly. Just heavenly," said Serpent. "But there was more," he added.

"More?" breathed Eve.

"As I ate, it seemed as if my eyesight, which previously could only distinguish light from dark, could now see glorious color. My ears could hear the songs of the stars, and my tongue could understand and speak the languages of the children. That meant that I could find you, Lady Eve, and tell you how much I adore you."

"Me?" said Eve in surprise. "Why not Adam? Or the angels? Or God?"

"Love does not choose, Lady Eve. It commands."

"Not a very reasonable answer," said Eve, who was flattered nonetheless. "But, Serpent, is this tree very far away?"

"No," said the Serpent. "It's quite close."

"Well," said Eve. "I, too, am hungry and thirsty. Can you take me to this tree?"

"I would like nothing better," replied Serpent.

Her Delight in Disorder

Chaos is violent and exhilarating! God, I can only say that experiencing the physicality of the universe outside Hell is striking, literally striking. It's so much more energetic than Hell, at least my corner of it. In my corner, I'd watched Death mope. I'd wondered how I could care so much for Death and be so indifferent to his siblings. I'd wondered why I didn't feel the same motherlove for them that I do for Death.

I'd remembered the dreariness of my shadowy existence under Satan's foot, the terror of my flight, the dread of discovering that I'd landed so far away from Home in what would be the cesspit of your creation with my very needy son, Death. To pass the Time, I'd imagined more companionship—first Satan and his cohort—then you and yours.

Then I'd started speculating about your children—whether they are any easier to raise than mine—but this was all in my imagination, so, God, imagine my surprise when, as I was imagining the Satan of my memory, Satan manifested like a bat out of the passageway and started threatening Death. He was bigger than I'd remembered, and filthier, soiled by contact with entropy and his own unbridled arrogance. He stank of anger and pride and lust. Until I entered Chaos, this was the closest I'd come to understanding the differences between the dreamed and the experienced, the imagined and the real.

The imagined and the real.

But that's not quite accurate, is it, God?

It's not *either* the imagined *or* the real, *either* here *or* there, but probably both *and* somewhere, someTime, in-between.

God, your ordered, harmonious, and dimensionless infinity existed prior to Time.

In Time, is it still there?

If it is, is it a memory or a reality?

If reality, whose reality is it?

Yours? Satan's? Mine?

Am I a projection of you? Or you of me? What if it's you who is now the character in search of an author?

How would I tell your story? And would the author of such a story even matter?

But what if I get the story wrong? What if it's only a Once Upon a Time story?

A myth?

A lie?

But I can't worry about that right now, because even as I tell this story, I experience the terror and exhilaration of Chaos. Here, in this spaceTime between Hell and Eden, between here and there, fly, float, or flop the raw matter and energy of all creation and transformation.

Even cataloging the contents of Chaos—particles& strings, waves&packets, quarks&quirks, atoms&molecules, composings&decomposings—implies an order, a narrative arc, an authority, Oh Author, that does not exist. Kinetic and potential energy compete, lacking any organizing principles of behavior. The transformations of matter and energy occur with bewildering suddenness, and yet, to me, there is a delight in such disorderliness.

In this space between good and evil I experience anarchy and wildness, but also all the potentiality that ever was, is, and can be.

Admittedly, God, the immediate shock of unfiltered sensation and stimulation stunned me silly. But it was all—ALL—so energizing after the eternal shadowy dullness of Hell (and what a fitting damnation that would be for a fizzy elemental like Satan—eternal dullness).

In Chaos light is experienced in all spectrums without any filtering by Time or media. The result is such a range of whites—eggshell, beige, cream, taupe, pearl, ivory, snow, ecru, and all the shades in between—that the whites themselves become a source of constantly shifting wonder. (As you know, God, you won't see much white in Hell. The closest might have been the fur of that baby goat, but even that was quickly befouled by the fearful contacts she'd experienced.) Now add random flashes of color that wink and then disappear in arcs or zigzags or dazzling afterimages.

In Chaos sound is unfiltered by Time or media. All is random and ambient. I had expected a clashing discord, as can be heard in Hell from the shrieks and moans of the damned, but instead, noise hisses gently, whitely, with sparks, arcs, and zigzags of squeals, groans, and pink grace notes.

In Chaos smell is experienced as random particles or subparticles coming together briefly as small molecules and then breaking up, but they can't be detected until they collect in sufficient numbers. One such collection constituted my waxed rope, which retained at least the memory of the stinky but reassuring umbilical cord to my child, Death.

God, you must be one Hell of a creator if you can encompass and order this glorious messiness into harmony and order as a Garden for your other children.

Save some of it for us.

I spend another moment or second or eon absorbing the energy of Chaos.

Then Time propels me toward our new Home.

Eve Takes the Bait

Serpent glided smoothly ahead of Eve, down the very same mint-strewn path she'd sown and that Adam had trampled earlier this morning. Was it really only this morning?

Odd, she thought. Although Adam didn't come here often, she certainly did. Wouldn't she have noticed a tree with red and gold fruits in this part of the Garden? What a great discovery this would be to share with Adam tonight! What kind of name might Adam choose for a tree whose fruits confer speech and heightened perception in those who eat from it?

Her stomach growled once more.

"How much further, Serpent?" she asked.

"Not far at all, Lady Eve. Just past this hibiscus, and, … there! You can see it there."

Eve stopped in dismay as Serpent indicated, with a flick of his tongue, the very Tree where she'd seen the sprites dancing some Time ago. The fruits now hung low enough even for a snake, or a sprite, to pluck, but surely these fruits were no more extraordinary than any other. *Or is it, perhaps, that, unlike Serpent with his enhanced perception, I cannot see the fruits in all their beauty?*

The moss under the Tree was deep green and velvety.

"Well, Serpent, you could have spared us this trip. This is the Tree that is forbidden for us to eat."

"Forbidden? How strange," Serpent replied. "Why is it forbidden?"

She hesitated before saying, slowly, "On the day we eat of its fruits, we die." She frowned in some perplexity. She'd understood "die" as an undesirable consequence, but that certainly didn't seem to be the case for Serpent, who shimmered with a vitality she hadn't seen in the other snakes in the Garden.

"You've read my mind, Lady Eve. Here I am before you, and if this is what 'dying' means, I'm all the happier for having done so. And I could never have expressed this to you had I not eaten the fruits of this tree. Does the tree have a special name?"

"The Tree of Knowledge of Good and Evil," Eve answered.

"'Tree of Knowledge,' hey? How very odd," Serpent mused, as if to himself. "Why would God and the angels want to keep 'Knowledge' from their beloved children, Adam and Eve?"

Perhaps Adam knows, but I don't. Should I have paid more attention to the warning? Should I have asked God and Raphael why? Are the fruits poisoned in some way? Intoxicating? And yet Serpent looks all the better for his experience. Which am I to believe, the warning from God and the angels and Adam or what my own senses show me?

"Lady Eve," Serpent said softly. "It is not my place to say, but..."

"But what?" Eve asked.

"May I speak freely?"

She nodded.

"Have you ever considered that God and the angels are testing you and Adam?"

"'Testing' us how?"

"To see if you're ready to join them as immortals."

"Why would we want to be immortals? We have our Garden, our journeys of birth and rebirth. Soon we will have our own children."

"So why else, then," Serpent asked softly, "would they make this prohibition against knowledge in this one particular area, when they are so anxious to have you learn in all other ways? See how eating the fruit has changed the perception of a lowly Serpent like myself. Perhaps 'dying' or 'Death' is the means by which you would become like the angels.

"No, it must be more than that," he said, rippling so that his scales shimmered. "Perhaps you would become like God themself!" Serpent paused, looking sorrowfully at Eve. "But, wait. Perhaps God does not want you to become like them, to join them as equals. Perhaps they want you to stay as you are under their thumb, without the freedom that they enjoy. Perhaps they want you to remain childlike, as their servants. Or, perhaps, . . ."

"'Perhaps' what?" whispered Eve.

"Perhaps the fruits will be given to Adam to eat so that he can become like them and you will remain as a servant to Adam as well as God and the angels. And then you can sing to their glory, all their glory, all the Time."

"I am so hungry and thirsty," Eve sighed.

"'Hungry and thirsty' for what?" asked Serpent.

"For food. For drink.

"For understanding."

"Then eat of the Tree," Serpent advised. "You will receive food, drink, and understanding. And glory and freedom as well."

She shook her head. "God has given us so much; why would they want to keep this one Tree from us when we can have anything, everything, else?"

Serpent shook his head also, the eyes glittering, then raised his head, as if he'd just thought a new thought. "Lady Eve, did you not see seven sprites dancing around the Tree some Time ago?"

"Yes, I did, Serpent. How do you know that?"

"Remember, Lady, I've loved and followed you all this Time. These sprites weren't always as you saw them, with humanlike speech and form. They were:

"a bear, . . .

"a peacock, . . .

"a pig, . . .

"a snake, . . .

"a frog, . . .

"a dog, . . .

"and a goat."

Eve frowned. "But then why are you not a sprite instead of a Serpent? And did you not tell me that you alone ate the fruits of this Tree?"

"Oh, a simple misunderstanding," said Serpent, quickly. "I meant to say that I alone am the speaker for the others."

"I see," said Eve, but she didn't. *Why then is Serpent a serpent and not a sprite? And why has he changed his story?* She stood. "Serpent, it has been a pleasant diversion to talk with you, but I will go elsewhere to seek refreshment. Good day to you."

"But . . . but wait, Lady Eve," said Serpent.

"Why?" asked Eve.

"I have more to say," said the Serpent. "If I may, Gracious Lady."

"You may."

"Lady Eve, you are the most beautiful and the most playful of God's children. Have God and the angels provided this prohibition as a clue in the most important of all games you and Adam may ever enjoy? Consider reasonable Adam and his approach to you and the Garden. Given the gift of designating, he has pleased God and the angels with all that he has named and accomplished.

"But you, Eve—given your understanding between what is and what could be, what have you accomplished?"

Eve studied the ground. Small grubs crawled in and out of the windfalls from the Tree. Had even they eaten from the Tree? She searched them for some sign of change, some hint that they were about to become butterflies without first having to cocoon. But she saw none. *They're only grubs, after all.* "There will be our children," she said. "Someday," she added.

"Yes, 'what could be,'" says Serpent. "Little Adam, Little Eve, and Little golden-eyed What's-its-name."

"How did you know??" Eve whispered, her eyes wide. She had not told anyone, not even Adam, about the third child. *But Serpent was following me, and perhaps he heard my song.*

"It's the fruit," Serpent said, as if he'd heard her very thoughts. "The eating of it has conferred great knowledge and insight upon a lowly snake like me. One can only imagine what it would confer upon you.

"God and the angels have provided you, and you alone, with a magnificent clue in this grand game that you are playing.

"I am that clue. If you do not learn from my experience, perhaps you do not deserve to take the next great turn in the game, to receive the gift of the 'Knowledge of Good and Evil.'

"Perhaps your place remains perpetually with the other Children like these," said the Serpent, as he flicked his tongue at the grubs and then, as if they were irresistible, swallowed them and gulped so quickly that Eve was not sure what she'd just observed.

What did register, however, was the new note of pity in Serpent's tone, along with a thread of something that she had not heard before—perhaps it could be called contempt. *It is a new game, as I thought. A new game for me! The clues have been here all along. Why shouldn't I play in this most ludic of experiences? Why shouldn't I show Adam the way? Take the lead for once?* "Please leave me, Serpent," Eve said majestically. "I have much to consider."

"As you wish, Gracious Lady." Serpent slithered away from the mossy bank, behind the hibiscus hedge, and onto the mint path, leaving a faint whiff of salt and sulfur, copper, iron, and ozone in his wake.

Alone with the Tree, Eve considered her next move in this most intriguing game. The sprites had sung of what is "more beautiful" and "less suitable." What a wonderful riddle. *Surely they must be part of the game as well. What Adam does with Raphael and his work is, of course, entirely suitable. And dutiful. But Serpent has regarded me as more beautiful. Dutiful can be hot and tiring and boring. Suitable remains a way to play the game safely, but, as Serpent has indicated, maybe "suitability" is not the right strategy here. This fruit, this food of the intellect. How beautiful it appears, moist and dewy. And how hot the sun shines.*

Her stomach growled once more. She felt the faint reminder in her thumb that only this morning, she had been pricked by the wild rugosa rose, which Adam had promptly relocated to a more "suitable" place. *A "suitable" place is fine for plants, but not for me.* She reached the hand with the pricked thumb toward the Tree, plucked a particularly juicy gold fruit. Its moisture stung the thumb briefly and then cooled it.

Susan W. Lyons

She bit into its moist, ripe flesh.
She trembled.
So did Eden.

She Is Surprised

Chaos trembles, and so do I. I can feel it to my core. The rope in my hands shivers. I pull it tight to rid the tremor, but then it goes briefly slack in my hands before it steadies.

What has happened?

I focus down the rope's length as far as I can see, which, of course, lacking a horizon or other reference, doesn't tell me what "far" is.

I stare, blinking against the shifting lights. Finally, I see a dark object about the size of a tooth.

I blink several Times. Amid the swirl of transformation around me, the object grows. It is moving, and moving fast.

Now amid the ambient noise I distinguish a thready wail, the pitch of which rises and falls even as it increases in volume.

The object is now visible as a gaping mouth. All that constitutes composings, decomposings, particles, quarks, or quirks, disappears into the maw, creating a brief negative space, like a shadow.

The shadow projects the shape of my son, Death.

The wail deepens to a roar.

Dear God, Death has left Hell.

What has happened?

He speeds past, leaving a red trail like a blood smear and waves of gravity that ripple in his wake, their apex pointing at the Garden.

I follow.

Eve's Eyes Are Opened

The first taste of the forbidden fruit was rich and creamy, but the second bite was cloying. Eve put the fruit down after the third bite. She closed her eyes to await the revelation or transformation or whatever it is she was supposed to experience, but that simply induced vertigo. She opened her eyes and very carefully sat down upon the mossy bank.

The serpent was nowhere in sight.

Neither was Adam.

What have you done, Eve?

The serpent told me eating the fruit would make me wiser and more godlike.

Why would you believe a talking snake?

It seemed like a good idea at the Time. She giggled before a wave of nausea made her put her head between her knees and moan. Eventually, she curled into a fetal position and fell asleep.

Eve awoke with a dull headache. She felt generally bloated, and her breasts and vagina in particular were tender and swollen.

What Time was it? She could not say. The sun was low in the horizon, but the sunset looked duller, grayer, than she would have expected. Was it going to rain? Even the air felt heavy. Where were the birdsong and angel chant that lullabied the days into evenings?

It was well past Time to return to Adam, but what would she have to say to her other self? What story would she tell? What would she do?

Eve raised herself stiffly from the ground, feeling strange aches in her joints. She walked over to the brook and splashed cold water on her face, gazing with bleary eyes at her reflection in the water.

A transformed Eve stared back, an Eve with dilated pupils, tangled hair, flushed cheeks, and swollen lips. Eve closed her eyes in shock, and then slowly opened them again.

She watched her lips compress to a thin line before curving into a knowing smile.

What did that smile know?

What did Eve know?

What did Eve know that Adam did not? *The knowledge of Good and Evil.*

Knowledge is power. Good to know.

Reluctantly, Eve pulled herself up and away from her reflection, stood, and began her journey home to Adam, her new knowledge revealed in the saucy little hip-roll that now governed her steps.

What Angels Think about Forbidden Fruit

If Raphael had a heart, it would burst with pain. "Why didn't I see this coming?"

God answers, "When we were We, We knew that We were eternal only until one of Us stepped away. We saw that coming, along with the beginning of Time, but that doesn't mean that we would, or should, have changed it."

"Let me at least warn Adam." Raphael stands and prepares to manifest.

"No, Raphael." God says. "We will not interfere in today's activities."

"But what part of 'forbidden' does this stupid child not understand?" asks Michael. "It's not as if Eve hasn't been warned again and again to leave that Tree alone. The commandment is clear and straightforward. Any tree in the Garden but that one. Any fruit in the Garden but that one. That is the ONE that is forbidden.

"For-bid-den.

"Taboo.

"Untouchable.

"What could be clearer?

"She'll bring disaster down on Adam."

Little Abdiel, who likes the company of the archangels and who has itself experienced Satan's rhetoric, is more sympathetic. "Satan has a wily tongue, and Eve has had no previous experience with fraud. Neither has Adam. Why wasn't this part of their education so that they could have armed themselves against Satan's ploys?"

God says, "Unlike we and Satan who existed before Time, Adam and Eve live *in* Time, in a perspective that knows 'was' and 'is' but does not know 'ever shall be.'

"They, unlike we, learn and grow in Time, along the paths of experience and education."

"So why *wasn't* this part of their education?" Raphael asks.

"What makes you think that this *isn't*?" God responds. "Wait.

"And watch.

"And we shall see what *shall be*."

Madam, I'm Adam

Adam would have talked to Raphael about Eve's peculiar attitude and alarming behavior during their encounter by the willows, but he sensed the angel would not necessarily agree with him that her attitude was peculiar and her behavior alarming. "You are complementary," he imagined the angel saying. "You are not meant to be mirrors of each other or agree with each other all the Time. You manifest distinct points of view and so you should expect to manifest different memories about your experiences."

Besides, Raphael had not appeared today. Adam was all alone.

And lonely.

Adam had raised his concern with God some Time ago. Why did Eve like to wander off? God nodded to indicate their understanding of Adam's question. Perhaps she wandered off because she, like Adam, still had some growing to do.

"Remember when we gave you the gift of Designator?" Yes, of course Adam remembered. "Have you shared it with Eve?" Well, not quite. Maybe some, but not entirely. After all, she hadn't seemed terribly interested. She'd rather play with the animals than name them. "Yes, well. Adam, it's a great responsibility to keep to yourself, because it means that only your point of view, not Eve's, goes into the naming. When you name an object or a child you affix it in Time. You recall it by name, but it's *your* perspective that has determined that name, not Eve's."

"Well, God, I discuss these designations with Raphael."

"*Well, Adam*, Raphael is fine, but why not with Eve as *well?*"

Well, certainly Adam had consulted with Eve on occasion. There was the "crabapple," for example.

"Were there other shared namings?" God asked.

Maybe one or two, but frankly, Eve didn't seem to have his facility with names, and when he tried to explain his system to her, she asked questions about why this phylum or why not that class. It was more bother explaining it to her than just keeping the classifications to himself. That's why *he*, not *she*, was the Designator, was it not? If she really cared, wouldn't she learn his system?

"Mmm," God had said. "Did you consult with Siffrhippus, Rhinoceros, Ape, or Dog before you named them?"

"Why would I?" asked Adam in surprise. "I, not they, am the Designator."

"What would it feel like, to be named Siffrhippus?" God asked.

That's the kind of question Eve would ask. What does it matter? "I don't know—small and horsy, I suppose. Does it matter?"

"It might to Siffrhippus," God said. "Do you still play with the animals?"

"No. Why should I? They have their own families now."

"Eve still plays with them."

"How childish," Adam had sniffed.

"She has learned much from them," God had responded.

Learn from beasts? Rhinoceros? Dog? Honeybee? Why not learn from me? Doubtless chirping with orioles instead of talking with me is why her thinking is so disordered, and this morning's disagreement over how to spend our day provides the simple proof of that. In fact she and I will have a serious talk this evening about the day's experiences.

After leaving Eve, Adam spent the late morning mulling the designation of mushrooms. Did they belong with mildew and mold, or did they need their own group because they were edible? Eve had told him about some molds that made cheese taste better, so would that count as edible? *Too bad she didn't stay by my side. I might have consulted her.*

Adam spent his midday in the shade under the arbor that Eve had woven from willow boughs. He ate grapes and wondered if the powdery mildew that dusted their skins contributed to their juiciness. *I might have asked Eve that question, were she here.*

Of course he could always ask God or Raphael that same question, but he wouldn't. Not today. Not now.

At the lake, he hunted, both Adam and Trout enjoying the hide and seek, the shivery pleasure of discovery, the capture. This particular trout, marked by a vivid red dorsal, had teased Adam for several days before surrendering for what would be its seventh or eighth journey of rebirth. Adam remembered the flesh from previous incarnations as firm and sweet, and the individual egg from which this trout would re-emerge as distinct from the rest of the roe.

He and Trout were playing, weren't they? *See, God? We're playing. At least I'm playing. I think Trout is too, unless he's thinking about the dragonfly he'd like to catch for dinner, or maybe about how his mate will feel without him, whether she will feel the same way I would if Eve took her own journey of rebirth without me.* Adam shook his head and wished God had not asked him about how the other children might *feel.* But, of course Trout's mate would *feel* differently from Adam because Adam and Eve, unlike Trout and his mate, were still the only two of their kind.

Then Adam considered turning this day into a version of hide-and-seek with Eve as the hider and Adam as the seeker, just to watch over her, certainly not to send her on a journey of rebirth and not even to interfere with what she was doing, of course, since that seemed to bother her. Adam just wanted to know what could possibly be of greater interest to her than he himself.

But then that would not be the honorable action to do, given their bargain. If she didn't know it was a game of hide-and-seek, then it would be more like spying, which *felt* to Adam like a creepy, slithering sort of behavior that required concealing oneself under bushes and moving stealthily and such.

His other self deserved better.

The early afternoon had a heavy, thundery feel to it. Cumulus clouds that ordinarily soared overhead—Eve had once said they were like cotton balls, but why settle for saying something was "like" instead of describing it accurately with the right name?—had given way to low and disordered stratonimbi in hues of gray, slate, smoke, dust, and ash. The air pressure had dropped as well. Adam napped under the shade of his and Eve's favorite cherry tree, until he was startled awake by the rumbling and trembling of the ground beneath him, followed by a shower of cherry blossoms that covered his body and reminded him of Eve's petal-softness, and, more painfully, of her absence from his side.

Eden had these quakes from Time to Time. Raphael said they were usually indications of a growth spurt.

At about sunset, when the shadows had lengthened, he prepared an evening meal under the arbor, taking great care to set out Eve's favorite foods: mushrooms picked from under a neighboring sycamore, that excellent trout, and a mix of purselane, dandelion, mustard seed, and pine nuts. He placed them on fresh fern leaves, and waited.

And waited.

As night fell, he scanned the path that he expected Eve to take, but a cloying fog had drifted in that veiled the stars and moon in a hazy light and distorted familiar objects. He thought the fog must be distorting sound as well, the normal night song echoing and buzzing in his ears instead of sounding the usual evening harmonies.

Most disconcerting.

Dis-concerting!

Hah! Good one!

He would remember to tell that to Eve.

Adam practiced to himself the story he would tell her of the day's events. He wondered if she'd felt the quake as he had. She would have enjoyed the shower of cherry blossoms.

It was really getting quite late. The ferns and greens wilted; the fish grew cold. Adam finally ate the trout himself. To delay its journey would be wrong.

Where is she?

He waited.

Adam heard Eve's voice before he saw her. "Adam, ADAM! Where are you, Adam? Call out to me and stay where you are until I can find you."

Adam heard the neediness in her call. She'd missed him. *Two can play at this game.* "I'm here, Eve. By the arbor," he said, hiding behind a laurel.

Eve came into view, gazing anxiously at the shifting shadows in the arbor. "I can't see you, Adam. Where are you?"

Now Adam could hear panic in Eve's voice. But he could hear something else as well. Something new. He watched.

She licked her lips and ruffled her hair. "Adam? Adam?" she cried, staring into the darkness, one hand on hip. She wheeled in a circle, eyes wide open, pupils dilated, trying to see invisible Adam. "Adam? Adam?"

He crept up behind her and tapped her on her shoulder.

She shrieked and jumped. "Oh, there you are!" she said. "How you startled me, Adam!" She took a few deep breaths, perhaps even a few more than she needed just to catch her breath.

Adam eyed the rise and fall of her breasts. In the mist, they glowed with beads of dew. Or perspiration. They looked like firm and ripe fruit. Oranges? Melons? He really had missed his Eve.

Adam watched Eve watching him watch her breasts. She licked her lips again and poked at her hair. Even in the half-light, her cheeks looked flushed, and she, like her breasts, was glowing. Strange new gestures and a strange new look, but Adam found them... found *her*... newly desirable.

"Adam," she said, in a breathy little voice. "I have so much to tell you."

"So come and tell me," Adam said. He took her by the arm and led her under the cherry tree. He swept aside the remains of dinner, and they sat.

She brushed Adam's thigh, as if absentmindedly, and began to stroke it. "Well, Adam, I know you must think I've been gone for too long, but it's been such an extraordinary day, and I hardly know where to begin."

"Begin at the beginning," he said, and his hand brushed her breast.

She sighed once more. "When you left me, I worked very hard. Very hard. At pulling weeds and vines and such." She continued stroking Adam. "Very hard, indeed," she murmured.

"Yes, Eve?" Adam rubbed Eve's nipple between his thumb and forefinger.

She leaned in. "So hard that I grew quite hungry and thirsty. But then a wise serpent came to me and told me where to find food and drink."

"A wise 'what'?" Adam asked in some irritation. He removed Eve's hand.

"A wise serpent," Eve repeated.

"How did you know it was wise?"

"It spoke to me."

"What, like the way you and the beasts speak?"

"No, Adam," and Eve's hand found its way between Adam's legs again, burrowing into his groin. "It spoke to me in our tongue."

Her own tongue peeked out between her lips. He moved his own hand back to Eve's nipple, pinching it until he saw her grimace. She placed her hand over his own until he stopped pinching her. Then she resumed the long, rhythmic strokes that were overriding all reasonable explanations for why she should not tell him this story…

… This myth.

… This lie.

He swelled with interest.

She resumed. "This serpent told me that he gained great wisdom and perception, as well as the ability to speak in our tongue," and here her own tongue peeked out once more.

Is it the shifting mist that makes her tongue seem to flicker? Adam was fascinated. No, that's not the right word. Adam was enthralled by Eve's … story. "Oh, and Adam?" Eve was saying, and her lips as they puckered over the "Oh" were moist and deep with promise. "This serpent told me that he and seven other children ate of the Tree of the Knowledge of Good and Evil. And you know what? They all became wiser, and the snake became the wisest and could talk to me."

Funny how much Adam's penis, when aroused, resembles a rampant cobra. "So, Adam," she purred, petting what she'd think of as *her very own serpent* until it shivered with desire. "I figured if the serpent could eat from the Tree of Knowledge of Good and Evil and grow wise, so could I. And so I did.

"I ate from the Tree."

Eve's pet serpent shriveled and hid. "What have you done, Eve?" Adam asked in terror. "What have you done?"

"I told you, Adam," Eve said impatiently. "I ate from the Tree of Knowledge of Good and Evil. And now my eyes are open."

"But why, Eve? Why would you disobey the one order we've been given?"

"Maybe you took only one order from the great Forbidder, but I've been taking orders from God AND you. 'Stay with me, Eve.' 'Don't be childish, Eve.' 'Don't eat the fruit from that Tree.' 'Don't talk to the beasts because they are beneath you.' 'Don't worry your pretty little head about my work.' Really, how many different orders am I supposed to be following here? Besides, if a snake can eat this 'forbidden' fruit and grow wise, then why shouldn't I?

"And of course, Adam, I did it for you."

"What?"

"Well, Adam," she sniffed. "I thought eating the fruit would make me more equal. And it has. The tree is not what we were told. Here I am before you, *and if this is what 'dying' means, I'm all the happier for having done so!* See?"

She slowly rose, uncoiling, performing an exotic little shimmy as she cupped her breasts and presented them in Adam's general direction. Still swaying, she bent until they were inches from his face and jigged them for Adam the way Adam jigged lures for Trout. "See?" she repeated softly. "The tree is not what we thought, Adam. I've eaten its fruits, and I live."

The pet serpent rose to the bait. But the rest of Adam did not. At least not yet.

"Foolish woman!" he said, and the pet serpent crept back into hiding. "What have you done to me? What have you done to *us*?"

Still now, and silent, Eve watched Adam. The next move in this great game was his. There was no turning back for her.

Adam put his head between his hands and thought. "Do not eat from The Tree of Knowledge of Good and Evil," God said. "On the day you eat from The Tree of Knowledge of Good and Evil you will die." *What does it mean to "die," anyway? If Eve does indeed die, as God said would happen to anyone who eats from this forbidden tree, and I do not eat from the tree, will God still take Eve away from me? Would I then be all alone, or would God make me another mate, another "other self"? Would this new self resemble my beloved Eve? Eve completes me, just as I complete her. How, then, can I live without her?*

I cannot.

Eve waited. And waited.

Finally, Adam raised his head and looked at his wife. "I see. Take me to the Tree, Eve," he said.

In the still swirling fog, the path toward the Tree was illuminated only by flickers and flashes that concealed more than they revealed. Adam heard the slithers and rustles of night creatures hiding as they came. *Odd, they've never hidden from me before.* Once, he stumbled over a root. The ground as he sprawled felt hard and unforgiving.

They reached the clearing. Eve plucked a fruit and gave it to Adam. Adam closed his eyes, took a deep breath, and bit into the fruit.

It tasted like ashes and dust.

Eden Tilts

The second tremor nearly yanks the rope out of my hands. It's as if Chaos has convulsed, but I have to ask what kind of energy could possibly organize Chaos sufficiently to disorganize it.

It would have to be a momentous matter, a matter of such moment as to alter spaceTime.

Where was my son Death going? What was his destination? And why? Only his terrible and terrifying hunger would drive him out of his familiar surroundings, and only if he thought he could satisfy that appetite.

Oh, God. OhmyGod.

It's Eden, isn't it?

Death has arrived in Eden and shaken its very foundations.

Adam's Eyes Are Opened

Adam opened his eyes and stared at Eve. He squinted, rubbed them, and blinked.

He opened his eyes again. Against the shifting light, she looked two-dimensional, this Eve, as if someone had traced her outlines and shown her only in primary colors. Most of her was white—garish and startling against the night's darkness, but her lips, breasts, hips, and bottom were outlined in blood red, as was her pubic hair. The effect was astonishing. Was this the knowledge Adam acquired from eating that wretched fruit? Or was the knowledge hidden somewhere inside those cartooned red lines?

He looked again.

Lips, breasts, hips, buttocks, pubes.

No, that wasn't right. It was really even simpler.

Tits, ass, and cunt.

That's what Eve was. The sum of her parts. And the sum of those parts had to add up to the secret knowledge.

She had it. He wanted it.

He fell upon her.

They copulated and fornicated and swyved and screwed and humped and sucked and fucked and boinked and banged and bonked. And, Adam thought, she tasted and smelled and felt like ashes and dust.

Inflamed, enlarged, enraged but still engorged, they went at it again. They tongued, licked, nibbled, and bit. They grabbed, clawed, pulled, pinched, punched, and tore.

They toed and kicked.

They panted. They glared.

They broke off momentarily to catch their breath. Then they went at it again. There was a secret knowledge out there, hidden in the experience of the other's body.

The body of the other, and they'd ransack every bulge, crook, crevice, and cranny until they found it and took it.

But they couldn't find it.

Finally, exhausted, drained, scratched, bleeding, covered in their own drying juices, Adam and Eve fell away from each other and retreated to opposite sides of the Tree of Knowledge of Good and Evil, with no sense of whose side was Good and whose was Evil, or even if there was any difference, let alone what might exist in the spaces between the two.

Frankly, at this point they didn't give a flying fuck.

They couldn't. They'd tried that once already and it hadn't worked.

Finally, spent, exhausted, empty, and drained, they slept.

They slept, badly.

They slept badly because the fruit of the Knowledge of Good and Evil roiled their guts and dried their mouths. They slept badly because, for the first Time ever, they experienced what it felt like to sleep away from each other. They slept badly, whimpering under the force of a new nightmare that a monster named Death had arrived in Eden who was hunting them now, even now, whose landing had shaken Eden to its very core, causing it to shudder and then careen some 20 degrees off its axis, tilting it toward chaos and entropy, unbalancing it until its days and nights of equal length, days of warmth and sun, and nights of refreshing breezes and gentle moisture would be replaced with a capricious atmosphere that would alter most of Eden's climate from one of benign harmony to a landscape of violent and unpredictable change.

Winds would shift. Thunder and lightning, sleet and snow, heat that seared or brought the landscape to a slow boil, ice, hurricanes, tornadoes, flooding, and earthquakes would erode Eden's landscape from Garden to Wasteland.

All would decompose.

What Angels Think about
Sin, Death, and Time

Raphael pleads with God. "We can't let Satan and Death win, God! Can we?"

God considers Raphael. "Why not? And it's odd Raphael, that you use the term 'win' as if this is a game about competition, with winners and losers, *eithers* and *ors*."

Raphael frowns. "We set the rules for Satan to turn it into one. Of course he would take advantage of the opportunity to do so. And, of course, he would cheat to win."

"You believe that Satan's cheating means that it was acceptable for Adam and Eve to disobey."

"Yes, I do," says Raphael, firmly.

Michael speaks. "And besides, we've already put too much energy, matter, and Time into those children to let them be swallowed up by Death."

"Swallowed up by Satan's foul words and their own desire for knowledge, a distinctive intellectual appetite bestowed by you, the Gift-Giver," amends Raphael.

"Besides," Michael continues. "I just can't stand the thought of how this story may end."

God surveys the angels in some surprise before addressing Michael. "So now it's a story, is it?" God says. "A 'Once-upon-a-Time' whose plot you'd like to edit?"

"The narrative to this point has demonstrated some potential," Michael concedes. "I've become accustomed to the children's ways, even Eve's. I'm curious to see what their children will be like, and that can't happen if they're all swallowed up by Death."

Raphael and Gabriel nod agreement.

"What about Sin?" God asks.

"What about her?" Michael answers. "Other than the fact that she's the mother of this monster that Adam and Eve have loosed upon Eden?"

"Sin is in Eden now," Raphael says. "And I believe she is hunting Death, just as Death is hunting Adam and Eve."

"She probably wants to find Death to make him all comfy and cozy in his new home in the Garden," Michael sniffs.

Raphael glares at Michael until Michael shrugs and looks away. "Sin has come alone, unprotected, of her own initiative, to slow her son's rampage through Eden," Raphael says. "I would think, Michael, that you of all archangels could admire her courage, if nothing else. Her importance to this story cannot be overestimated. Right, God?" Raphael asks the Author, less certainly.

God remains silent.

"She didn't choose Satan for her father/husband and Death for her son/husband," Michael concedes. "And she seems to be developing a change of heart, if it can be said that Sin has a heart to change. Perhaps I'm being a little hard on her, but really, with that name, how else can I think about her?"

"No 'perhaps' about it," Raphael says. "You *are* too hard on her. Sin denounced Satan and wants to come Home. What more could be asked of her?"

"That she change her family name, if not her family?" suggests Michael.

"But she wants to bring Death with her to live with us," God says. "And Death and we are incompatible."

"Incompatible here, but not in Eden," Michael responds. "In fact, we assured Adam and Eve that on the day they ate of the fruit of the Tree of Knowledge of Good and Evil they would die. They ate the fruit; ergo now they are going to die."

"How do we know that?" Gabriel asks quietly. God and the other archangels look at him expectantly. Gabriel rarely vocalizes. "I mean," he continues, "we know that Adam and Eve will die, and we know that it will happen as a consequence of the choices they made. But, what does 'to die' mean?"

"I suppose," Raphael muses, "it means that they'll cease to exist. Won't they?"

"But what would that be like, to 'cease to exist'?" Gabriel persists. "Would the heart stop?"

"Yes, it would," God replies.

"So Time would stop as well?"

"For the one whom Death has taken, yes," God replies. "Not for anyone else, naturally."

"I don't understand," says Michael.

God nods to Gabriel to continue. "Time is tempo as well as narrative. Tempo takes us from what was to what is and to whatever shall be as well. We measure tempo in the lub-dub of the heart. When the lub-dub stops for anyone, so does the heart. When the heart stops, so does tempo. So, therefore, does Time."

"But these are children who were created to be born and reborn inside of Time," Raphael says. "What happens to them when they're swallowed by Death, their hearts stop beating, and they're taken out of Time?"

"We are beings out of Time, are we not, Raphael?" God says.

"We are," Raphael agrees. "If Death stops Time for the children, taking them out of Time, can they then come Home to us?"

"Potentially. If they choose to," God says, manifesting a collective shrug.

The angels ponder.

"But Satan is also a being out of Time," Michael says. "And Time has certainly marked him." The angels nod their agreement.

"Satan has chosen not to come Home," says God. "Time has marked him accordingly with entropy and decay."

"So Death cannot take him, but Time can?"

"Time frames yesterday, today, and tomorrow," says God. "Time requires vocabulary, like 'past,' 'present,' 'future,' inside a narrative journey marked by memory, experience, and expectation. The great Dis-integration marked the fragmentation of wholeness into fractiousness, factions, and individuality. Satan has constructed an individual point of view that includes his unique memory of the great Dis-integration, his present experience with attempting to manufacture power, and his future expectations of success. As long as he remains trapped within these parameters, he remains trapped in Time."

"Is Time organic?" Michael asks.

"Time makes the organic possible," responds Raphael.

"Is Time subject to its own rules of entropy and decay?"

"Time is the agent of change," God says. "Like a mother, Time births change," he adds.

"Is Time a she?" Michael asks.

"Does it matter whether Time is gendered or an engenderer?" God answers.

"Well," responds Raphael. "It strikes me that Sin, a complex character in her own right, is so very different from her father Satan. I've wondered how, if he engendered her on his own, she would be capable of motherlove, let alone growth and change. I'd thought that maybe Satan had given her his better self. But now I wonder..."

"Yes?" says God.

"Now I wonder if Sin could somehow be Time's daughter as well as Satan's."

"Time's oldest daughter, she would be," God muses.

"Fine," says Michael. "Well and good. Sin is the daughter of Time as well as Satan. Great theoretical discussion, but I repeat my initial question: What's going to happen to Adam and Eve now that Death is loose in the Garden?"

"Time will tell," says Gabriel.

The Day After, Relatively Speaking

Adam and Eve awoke mid-afternoon with headaches, nausea, and a terrible sense of thirst and longing. They glared at each other through miserable, bloodshot eyes. "Cover yourself, Woman," Adam growled. "Your nakedness is disgusting and shameful."

Eve didn't answer, but slowly stood up, swaying a little as she did so, and tottered to the brook where she drank and drank the cold water. Then she stepped into the center of the brook, squatted, and tried to bathe away the evidence, if not the experience, of her new knowledge. Next, she searched for, and found, the fig tree she'd trellised only last week (or was it yesterday or a minute ago or before the beginning of Time?). Its ripe purple hanging fruits reminding her of Adam's recently engorged scrotum, with unnecessary roughness she twisted several of the large broad leaves off the lower branches and returned to the Tree of Knowledge of Good and Evil, where Adam was trying, unsuccessfully, to crawl on hands and knees to that same brook. Folding one of the smaller leaves into a shallow bowl, her hands still trembling, she scooped some water, approached him, knelt beside him, and offered him a drink.

He cupped her hands in his to sip the water that was still pure and cold. He closed his eyes, and drowsed. When he opened them again, his horizon resettled. "Thank you for the water, Eve," he said, finally. "Now we know how Waxwing and Unicorn must have felt."

Susan W. Lyons

"And now we know Good and Evil as well," Eve said. "Knowledge hurts."

"Let us cover our nakedness," Adam said. "It shames me."

Eve found an acacia tree whose thorns had been hollowed out by ants. Plucking one of the larger thorns and gently shaking out its inhabitants onto the tree trunk, with another thorn she bored a small hole in the base to make a needle. Next, she followed a Red Admiral butterfly to a stinging nettle, where she pinched several stems, removed them, and began to strip the leaves. Her hands itched and swelled from the toxins in the nettle, and she felt flaring pain now, as well. "Knowledge hurts," she reminded herself. After she'd stripped the leaves, she ran her needle along the nettle's stem, creating a slit. She opened the stem and pulled out its fibers, threading them through the needle. Returning to Adam, she sewed a skirt of fig leaves and tied it around her waist. After watching her, Adam did the same for himself. *What a novel sensation, to cover that which identifies our complementary natures.*

They tried hard not to look at each other, particularly at the skirts, which might as well be flaming orange for all that they advertised what Adam and Eve did not want to see, at least at this Time. Adam studied the brook instead. The water level had risen slightly, and the rushing water had gained opacity. In the shadows of the late afternoon, the brook looked muddy.

Eve tracked the flight path of a cohort of withered leaves of the Tree of Knowledge of Good and Evil as they floated to the ground. The Tree's canopy had thinned and the fruits were dropping as well. They smelled musty.

Finally, if not inevitably, Adam and Eve met each other's eyes.

"What did we experience last night?" Adam asked. "Why? If only you'd stayed with me, Eve, as I'd asked, none of this would have happened."

"You mean never parted from you? Stuck to your side like an extra rib? So I could listen to you and Raphael discuss *order* and *duty*?"

"You make those words sound dirty," Adam said. "But it's what we did last night to each other that feels dirty to me."

"Why do you think what we did last night was dirty, Adam?"

"Because what we did was . . . disobedient and disorderly."

"All of it?" Eve asked. "Or just some of it? I thought some of it was fun, like a new game. Without any rules."

"Right. Without any rules. Un-ruly," Adam said. "Un-ruly, disobedient, and disorderly."

"What I don't get, Adam," Eve said, "is why have rules at all if you're not going to enforce them. If it was so important to you that I stay right by your side, why didn't you just keep me there? You could have . . ." She broke off at the sound of rustling wings and rumbling Joy approaching. It was evening, and God and the angels were walking in the Garden.

Adam saw a panic in Eve's eyes that mirrored his own. They scrambled away from the Tree and took cover in the hibiscus hedge.

"Adam, Eve. Where are you?" came the rumble.

Silence.

But of course there's no point in trying to hide from God.

"Uhmm, we're here, God," Adam said, stepping out from the shelter of the hedge. Eve slowly followed, making herself as inconspicuous as possible behind Adam. Pollen from the hibiscus blossoms stuck to their hair and aprons, dusting them gray in the evening light.

God looked at them quizzically. "Is this a new game you're playing?"

"No," said Adam.

"Were you hiding from us?"

Adam nodded.

"Why?"

"This woman and I heard you coming. We were afraid because we're naked. And so we hid."

"Who told you that you were naked?" asked God.

Adam looked at Eve, who looked at the ground. The silence lengthened. He finally shrugged. "We just knew, that's all."

God said, "A strange new knowledge, to be sure. And how did you come to acquire this knowledge?"

More silence.

God persisted. "Did you eat from the Tree of Knowledge of Good and Evil?"

"You already know, God. Why ask us?"

"We want to hear you tell us why."

Adam looked at the ground, and then at Eve, and finally at God. "That woman gave me fruit from the Tree, and I ate it."

God turned their gaze to Eve. "Eve?" they asked.

Eve looked at God as if mesmerized. Finally she whispered, "A snake told me to taste the fruit."

"Really?" asked God, gazing at them both for an instant, or an eon, or both.

Then he regarded Adam. "'That woman'? Has Eve now lost her name, then, Oh Great Designator? Do you now use the gift of naming, or withholding a name, as a blunt instrument for degradation?"

Then God regarded Eve. "You took advice from a snake? Did all your careful and empirical observations of the creatures and plants of Eden desert you in the face of a *talking snake?*"

Then God regarded them together. "And after eating the fruit of this Tree, what did you learn about experiencing the Knowledge of Good and Evil?"

They shrugged, miserable in their new knowledge.

Knowledge hurt.

Satan Tries to Have the Last Word

"This next confrontation will not be any easier, will it, God?" says Michael.

"Satan gloating about his victory in the Garden?" asks Gabriel.

"Let him gloat," says God. "He has little Time left in the present tense."

"I see what you mean," says Michael, who cheers up considerably at the sight of Satan, who seems to be having difficulty shedding his scales and regaining his wings.

"Satan," hails God. "You seem pretty pleased with yourself. Are you enjoying this peculiar day?"

Satan hobbles to a halt and grins, but as he speaks, his tongue flickers uncertainly. "This day has been absurdly delightful, and God, I'm not just being spiteful. I've turned Adam and Eve into two who believe that out of great Good can come Evil."

God nods. "It's true you've inserted a plot wrinkle or two to complicate this great narrative arc."

"Are you kidding me? 'Wrinkle'? Call it a fractal. Give me credit," Satan says. "Soon Adam and Eve will be dead, and all Eden will then be instead my own pleasure palace richly furnished with malice and devilish spawn proudly bred."

"But, Satan, how do you know that all that you do does not simply burnish the luster and gleam of this first of all the great stories?"

"This great story? This great myth, you mean. Or perhaps, simply, this great lie," Satan replies. "You're quite the eternal optimist if you think any good can come of this. I'm telling you I've won, and your story is done. Evil is now quite victorious."

"And that's your final word?" asks God. "You don't want to come back to us?"

For an instant, or even a moment, Satan shows a great hunger, a great yearning, and God can see glimmers of the former light bringer. But then Satan squares what shoulders he has left. "Oh my God!" he hisses. "Don't you get it? You've lost! I've won! Get over it!"

God answers, "Once upon a Time was the beginning of the word as it was, is, and shall be." They pause, and add, softly, "Or could be."

Gabriel imagines musical fugues twisting themselves into elegant and precise love-knots.

Raphael imagines whorls of glorious fractals spiraling across spaceTime.

Satan imagines nothing and turns his back for the last Time. "All right, all right," he says. "Have it your way. Believe what you want. I'm off for one last farewell tour of Hell before retiring in, shall we say, a slightly used Garden of delights."

"We will miss you, Satan," says God softly.

Identifying Fractures and Fault Lines

Dear God, my son Death has landed in Eden, and his path is terrifyingly easy to follow. I see where his footsteps have burned the plains into deserts. Death has harvested the grasses and grasshoppers, sunflowers and sloths, smilodons, mammoths and woolly rhinos and elk and all that grow, creep, hop, stride, or run through the savanna, all living things in his path.

Scraping one talon along the terrified ground and gouging the gorges and canyons that will tattoo Eden, Death has excavated burrows, holes, dens, lairs, and warrens and scooped up their inhabitants, who squint in the sudden sunlight and then close their eyes tightly against the end of the world as they know it.

All, all have found their way down his gullet.

Death has splashed through the sea, boiling away the waters in his wake such that newly steamed and salted krill and leviathan, squid and seaweed, float to the surface, where he drinks, crunches, or munches them up, all up.

In the forest, Death has roasted mighty oaks and cedars, giant ferns, aneurophytes, moss, and redwoods, along with the mice, squirrel, bear, panthers, deer, wolves, siffrhippi, and their big cousins the horses who neigh their astonishment even as they are tossed into that maw.

Flapping his wings to create a tornadic downdraft, Death has swept pterodactyls, parrots, sparrows, hummingbirds, and the high-flying eagles into his mouth and savored the flesh of the creatures of the air.

Death has wrought all this havoc, and more.

However, dearest God, wreaking havoc takes a lot of energy, especially for a growing boy like Death, who eventually finds himself winded, if not yet sated, in this first full indulgence of his appetite, so not only is it easy to follow Death's destructive path, it's increasingly easy for me to catch up to him.

It takes me a few moments before I can distinguish between the screams of outrage from Death's dinners and the generalized roar of his excitement.

A violent gray tunnel of activity rises from the ground far into the sky. Death is the vortex of that tunnel. I can see that he's now massively bloated from this unaccustomed exercise and food. Boulders, dirt, and other inedible debris from his activity fly about him in an aerial whirlpool or lie strewn on the ground like Eden's bones.

I draw nearer until I can distinguish his form and then his features. Positioning myself directly behind him, I take my slingshot out of its sack, load a skull, aim low, and send him crashing to his knees.

The second skull from my bag hits him just at the coracoid process where his wings attach to his neck. His wings stop flapping. Slowly, Death collapses face-forward onto the ground and lies still. The ground trembles beneath him from the impact. Fractures and fault lines run in a giant cobweb pattern from under his massive body.

The winds subside; the shrieks fade away.

Eventually, God, there is a welcome silence, broken by the snoring of my son Death and punctuated with the belching and farting of argon, neon, and less noble gases like sulphur dioxide and methane, as well as water vapor, into the air. Death contributes to these emissions, of course, as he digests a small continent's worth of protein and fiber, but I also see vents in the new fractures around him exhaling in their own sighs and groans. The air shimmers and stinks with each wave of effluvia, but the gases themselves quickly disperse. The water vapor accumulates until it falls as dew into and around the vents and fumeroles.

Puddles form.

Death visibly deflates as he sleeps off the effects of his first and biggest banquet ever. The bloat subsides along with his monstrous growing pains.

That's my boy.

Quite the appetite, isn't it, God?

Of course by now you know that he gets that from his father, Satan, and not from me. But once you acquire that taste for fresh food, eating siblings in Hell is just so much less appetizing than dining on fresh food from the Garden. Not that I want to make any excuses for what has happened here, God, but wasn't it you who set up the entry of Death into Eden once Adam and Eve ate of the fruit of the Tree of Knowledge of Good and Evil? Again, not that I want to blame you.

In fact, God, we have common ground here. Satan tricked your children and teased mine into behaving badly. Satan himself must be quite bloated with pride at the current state of affairs: Eden in ruins, Death on the hunt for your children. The Master of Disaster! I'm done with him. He started this whole living in Time business, but it looks like Death may end it.

And what a shame that would be.

I sit by my son, stroking the wrinkles out of his brow. In Eden's clean air, his skin clears even as his features soften. Something like peace transfigures his countenance. I can now see his resemblance to me as well as to his father.

I know Home is where my heart should be, but I have to say that Eden is quite the lovely rest stop, God. I can see why Death was in such a hurry to get here. In fact, I would be more than content to sit here forever with my now quietly napping son and savor the pleasure that is the Garden. As amazed and exhilarated as I was by Chaos, so much more do I feel that Eden is a Garden of joy, even etched in the fractures and fault lines that delineate its fallen state.

In my imagination, Eden was an arranged and manicured landscape of order and harmony with not a blade of grass out of place, protected by a dome of sun, moon, and stars from the ravages of Time, Satan, or Death. But, God, I now see that order does not have to be regimental and that "dome" is not the right image. A dome keeps others out, but at the expense of confining those under its protection, its shell. What you've provided is a canopy that shelters against the physical elements, but, for better or worse, admits others, including Satan and his seven deadly children, as well as Death and me, into this beautiful world.

I might assume as a result that your purpose was to test your children by letting them fall prey to Satan's slimy rhetoric, discover their fractures and fault lines, find them disobedient, and then punish that disobedience. But that assumption doesn't fit with what I see, which is a glory of abundance, variety, and diversity in all life forms, even in Eden's current devastated state. How on Earth, God, were you able to imagine such a magnificent creation into existence?

And, God, even tilted on its axis, open to entropy and chaos and subjected to my son's rampage, Eden remains breathtaking. Inspiring. Dare I say that its fractures and fault lines frame the beauty that remains? That the evil frames the good?

As Death slumbers, I observe new life creeping out of the fault lines, as if Death's wild energy has regenerated Eden's womb. Time and Ge work together. At first the evidence is small and hard to see: archaea and then bacteria, some of which thrive but most of which fall prey to Death, who, even asleep, manifests appetite. Eukaryotes, algae, and protists follow. Some crawl into the puddles formed by the vents in the fault lines.

Now, even as Death inhales some in his sleep, others fly or float away and thrive.

Gymniosperms, angiosperms, fungi, sponges and worms, jellyfish and snails, sea-stars, and arthropods march, crawl, swim, climb, float into sight.

Can Adam and Eve be far behind?

It's been a long day, relatively speaking.

Adam and Eve Prepare to Meet Death

Adam and Eve were alone in the Garden.

God, Raphael and the other angels left them alone with their new knowledge.

Knowledge hurt.

And it made one lonely. *Singular word, "one," securely imbedded inside the walls of "lonely."*

"Where is God? Where are the angels? I do not think that I can stand the pain of their absence," Adam said to Eve.

"It hurts like the new knowledge," Eve replied. "But we are not alone, unless we want to be. We have each other," she added.

"Yes," agreed Adam. "We do have each other. That's what we chose."

"Did we choose wrong?" Eve asked anxiously. "Will we ever know? How would we know?"

"We know what God and the angels told us," Adam said. "And we chose otherwise. We chose to experience Knowledge of Good and Evil. That's what we chose. We chose us over them. Whether that's good or evil, who can say?"

"But what if it's not good *or* evil? What if it's both good *and* evil?" Eve asked.

"So what if it is *and* and not *or*?" Adam asked.

"If we've experienced good and evil, then both are embodied in us, as our children will be."

"Our children," Adam echoed. "Will we ever even have children? Will we have room for them now that we've chosen good and evil? What if we are alone, without children or God or the angels? What if there is now only us? And Death?"

"There is the Garden," Eve reminded him.

"Yes, but the Garden will change. It *has* changed. There is mud in the brook. Some of the trees are shaking and losing their leaves. The horizon is black with dust. I see lightning and hear thunder many Times louder than Smilodon's roar. "I had a terrible dream," he continued. "I dreamed that a monster named Death was loose in the Garden."

"I dreamed the same," Eve said. "I dreamed Death was coming for us. He roared louder than thunder."

"Death *is* coming for us," Adam said. "He smells us. He smells our fear. He smells our experience."

"What will he do when he finds us?" Eve asked, trembling.

"He will devour us, and that will be the end," replied Adam.

"No rebirth?"

"No rebirth."

"No Garden? No Home?"

"No Garden. No Home."

"But what about the good, the evil, and our children?"

"There will be no good, no evil, no children. We'll be all, all swallowed up."

They fell into each other's arms and cried for each other, for their children, for their new knowledge. They cried as if their hearts were broken.

And perhaps they were. Broken, that is. *Or at least cracked wide enough to now admit good AND evil, along with, of course, the children, if they didn't first run out of Time.*

"If only you'd listened to me instead of that snake."

"If only you'd listened to God instead of me."

Adam and Eve glared at their other self, ready to rend and tear each other apart again. They bared their teeth like wolves and arched their hands into claws. She hissed like a snake. He grunted like a boar. Then Adam sighed and closed and opened his hands until they relaxed and fell naturally to his side. "'If only' doesn't undo what's been done. Time has pushed us past 'what was.' Now there's only 'what is' and 'what shall be.'"

"What shall we *be* ...? What shall we *do* with our new knowledge then?" Eve asked, and she too relaxed into thoughtful sadness. "Can Time give us only 'shall be,' or is there also 'can be'? What future choices will we have? God can help us decide, if we ask, but will they?"

"Perhaps," agreed Adam. "But it's very hard to ask if they're not here."

Adam and Eve trudged to their arbor, said their prayers (how strange to talk to God without seeing them), and fell into each other's arms in a quiet and dreamless sleep.

More leaves fell in the night, blanketing Adam and Eve against the now-chilly air. The next morning, they awoke refreshed. The sun was out, revealing a fine lace of frost that glittered and winked in the morning light. The birdsong was back, but the angel chants were absent.

Adam gazed at the fallen and dying leaves that had sheltered them against the long night. Eve followed his gaze, and then they both looked up at the trees from which more leaves were falling. Some were brown and withered, but others had transformed from green to russet, gold, yellow, and orange.

"The leaves are dying," Adam said. "But their colors are more vivid than they were, like an early sunset."

"They are," agreed Eve. "Is this what dying will be like for us?"

"What was dying like for Serpent?" Adam responded. "What you saw might have been Serpent in a brief, colorful show, like the dying leaves."

"Where is Serpent?" Eve asked. "Why haven't we seen him?"

"Perhaps Death has found him," Adam answered.

"Let's find out," said Eve. "Let's hunt for Serpent and see if he can tell us anything more about Death." She hesitated. "No, let's not. Even if we found him, I wouldn't believe what he says anyway. In fact, just thinking about the sight and feel of him, or a snake, any snake, makes me shudder."

"All right, then," Adam said. "Eve, let's search out Death instead. Maybe I can wrestle him into submission. Maybe he's only a trickster like Serpent. Maybe he can be reasoned with. Maybe he doesn't want both of us."

"Adam, I was the first to disobey God. If I offer myself up to Death, maybe God will be satisfied and give you a new mate, a new other self with whom you can have children."

"Nonsense, Eve," said Adam firmly. "It is you who will bear our children, so it is you who will need to live. Death can take me if he is unreasonable,

"... *and* mightier than me,

"... *and* all that hungry."

"Let's go meet Death together," said Eve.

"It's Time," agreed Adam.

The Angels Study the Birds and the Bees

Raphael is so angry and agitated that its feathers stand on end until it resembles a giant baby snow owl. Michael would ordinarily laugh to see Raphael in such a state, but the angel can appreciate Raphael's response to Adam and Eve's utterly ridiculous idea that they should go meet Death.

"This has been the problem all along," Raphael storms, sparks of energy creating an electrical corona around its feathers. "Adam and Eve are sinking deeper and deeper into the folly of their self-absorption to the exclusion of considering the impact of their behavior on everyone else. How can they admit good if they're already full of themselves?

"We could have straightened Eve out about Satan as Serpent if she'd only asked us instead of trying to figure it out by herself! We could have told Adam that we would keep Eve safe for him, that he didn't have to choose between Eve and us!

"Why won't they trust us to help??"

Michael nods vigorous agreement. "Running to meet Death. What willfulness! What hubris, to think that they can solve this on their own! As if God would be 'satisfied'!" The angel spits the word out. "That's the very word Eve used, isn't it—'satisfied'—by their throwing themselves away as some sort of sacrificial offering. What do they take us for? Evil?"

"Not evil," God says. "Bees. Adam and Eve are thinking like the honeybees, who will meet and attack a threat from another even if it means sending themselves on an early journey to rebirth. They do it to protect their hive, their Home. And because they believe they are created in our image, they think of us as bees, too."

"But we aren't bees, and neither are Adam and Eve," Michael says.

"It's true we aren't bees," God says. "But we have given them some of our own cherished characteristics—collective thinking, a desire for harmony and stability, the yearning for Home, the desire to protect it from destruction by the other."

"When bees charge out to protect their home, they face early rebirth—or at least that's the way it used to be—but Adam and Eve now face Death," Raphael protests. "The two are not the same."

"Yes," God answers. "We promised Adam and Eve that if they ate of the fruit of the Tree of Knowledge of Good and Evil, they would die. And they did taste of it. And so they shall—die, that is."

"Why did we promise them that?" asks Michael.

God is silent for some Time. "Consider how our fluffiest of birds, the snowy owl, is born."

Apparently God *has* noticed Raphael's resemblance as well, thinks Michael, and the angel smiles to himself, but then he sees what God suggests and blurts out a response. "Born as an egg, the baby owl must hatch, must break out of its shell before it can live in the world!"

God nods. "And why, our beloved?"

"Because it needs more room than that which is supplied by the shell. The shell confines the growth." Michael stretches his wings to illustrate a glorious expansion of his own space.

"Indeed!" God agrees. "The shell starts as a cozy Home, but if the baby is to grow and thrive, it must break through into a larger world."

"Speaking of 'growing,'" Raphael asks. "What are we to make of what Sin calls Death's 'growing pains'? 'Monstrous growing pains'?"

Michael has been thinking more about the birds and the bees, but in particular about the birds. "In order to grow, the baby has to become uncomfortable enough in its egg to want to peck its way out. Pain is a sign of discomfort that leads to change, and, one hopes, growth. To 'growing pains.'"

"Yes, Michael," replies God. "You have perceptively distinguished between change and growth. Satan has changed, but he has not grown, and he has therefore deteriorated over Time until only pride, greed, and envy keep him from collapsing in a disorderly heap."

"Sin said that Satan, too, is a sign, that he was the original Sign," Raphael adds.

"And the original Sin," God says. "Satan is also the original Sin, the originating sign of the separation and fragmentation of wholeness and unity, of the fracturing of Home."

"'Sin,' 'Sign,'" sighs Michael. "More games with words."

"*Ludic* games with words," God amends. "Unlike the nasty word games Satan has played, ludic games will help our children name and remember their experiences in Time. Experience will also teach our children how to find the path Home, where 'Once upon a Time' transforms into *what was*, *what is*, and *whatever shall be*. Or *could be*.

"Satan's daughter has found her way to us along such a path; she has become a Sign that such a path, such a narrative arc, exists."

"She may be Satan's daughter," Gabriel reminds them, "but she is Time's daughter, too. We and Satan's daughter are different from Adam and Eve. Growth, like change, occurs over Time. And if—no, now it's *when*—when Adam and Eve run out of Time, they will also cease to grow."

"We must be certain, then, that our children do not meet Death before their Time is up," Michael muses.

Michael's use of "our" does not go unnoticed, or unappreciated, by Raphael and Gabriel.

"And now rather than allowing Adam and Eve to rush toward Death, let us consider how our efforts can cause good to come out of evil," says God. "And let us invite Satan's daughter—Time's daughter, I should say, for she has repudiated his authority—let us invite Time's daughter, who, like Adam and Eve, has experienced Satan's malice, to join us in this greatest of endeavors."

And so they do.

Time's Daughter and the Angels Find Common Cause, Relatively Speaking

"So are we cousins, then, Michael?" I ask the angel. He steps back, raising his wings and sword as if to ward off an imminent attack. "Don't worry," I say. "I'm just looking for a companion for my son Death—maybe someone he can go fishing with. I won't try to take any other advantage of the family tie, unless, of course, you'd like me to."

I smile sweetly.

As Michael pictures an afternoon, or a minute, or even a second spent alone with Death, the startled look on his face petrifies into fear, which, I admit, gives me pleasure. After all, how often can one catch Michael with his sword up but his guard down?

"She's teasing you, Michael," says Gabriel. "Another form of play."

"I am teasing you, Michael," I admit. "But perhaps I shouldn't, at least until we know each other better, even though I think Death would be so much better for knowing that he has family other than his father Satan. Relatively speaking, we could say."

"That will be a good conversation for another occasion," says God. "Our immediate purpose is to prevent the un-Timely meeting of your son Death with our son Adam and our daughter Eve."

Michael tries a small smile, more grimace, really, although I appreciate the effort. I return the smile—a real smile—this Time.

God and the angels have manifested in Eden, where I sit with Death, who rumbles and snorts his way through what has turned out to be a very long afternoon nap. Around him and through the vents he has created by the force of his own fall emerge platypi, crocodiles, anteaters, and frogs. A small pack of velociraptors clambers out next, sending the others scurrying away.

God and the angels watch the activity fondly. Raphael points out that the raptors look like small cousins of Death. I nod politely, because any expression of kinship among my branch of the family and that of the angels is a positive sign; however, I myself believe Death has become much more personable, or at least less saurian, in the last eon or so.

I, too, have already felt its healthy effects myself as the fresh air of Eden erases the ravages of Hell. Here, Time is a gentle friend, again relatively speaking.

"So," Raphael finally begins the discussion. "Death has created quite the mess, hasn't he?"

"How would he have learned any different, starved as he was for company and nourishment? All the young children in Eden have had more than enough food and guidance and companionship. Death has had only me and a barren Hellhole." I say hotly, remembering that while the heavenly host fought and played together, Death and I fought alone. But then I also recall the elementals and primordials who visited with me, taught me about love and waiting, and then encouraged me to find my own way out. And I learned from them. And now the more ignorant—or innocent, if that's the preferred term—among these angels, if they choose to, can learn from me.

For Death's sake, if not my own, I take a deep breath of relatively pure, fresh air. "But I should remind you," I continue, "that Death did not come to Eden on his own initiative. He was summoned by Adam and Eve when they ate of the fruit of the Tree of the Knowledge of Good and Evil."

"True," says Raphael, smoothly. "But it was your father, Satan—was it not?—who tricked Eve into breaking the rule that allowed Death entry into Eden."

"True," I agree. "It was my father, whom, as you well know, I have repudiated. But, of course, it is God—is it not?—who set that prohibition in place." Death snorts, as if in agreement, and rolls over on his back. Still sleeping, he inhales gustily, swallowing several auks, two moas, and a turkey, all of whom have attempted to loft themselves into the air above his head in what can only be described as a Death wish. He sneezes, ejecting the turkey, who flaps its wings and barely escapes Death's next downdraft. I smile fondly at Death and nudge him onto his side, where he settles agreeably back to sleep at the mortal expense of some slow-crawling tetrapods and salamanders.

We exchange further niceties, followed by a companionable silence. "So this is a family conference?" I ask.

"Yes," says God.

"Yes," agree the angels, even Michael.

"A family reunion," I clarify.

"Yes, a reunion. We take your point, Sin," says Michael. "We're all one family here."

"Including Death?" I ask.

"Including Death," answers God. Michael rolls his eyes and sighs.

"Why is it only the angels and not the primordials from the other branches of the family who were invited?" I ask. I admire Ge, the little I've seen of her, and had thought we might have much to say to each other. God says something about minor differences of opinion over what constitute good and evil, but I can see the question itself is enough to make them squirm. Perhaps, at a later reunion, this will be a conversation that includes more voices about whether the nature of good and evil changes over the course of Time.

"Yes, well, on this occasion we meet to discuss our *mutual* concern about the consequences of an unTimely meeting between Death and his cousins Adam and Eve," Raphael points out.

"Agreed," I say. "Now, as to the matter of an unTimely meeting, why on Earth are Adam and Eve even attempting to meet Death? Aren't they aware of the consequences?"

"Because they're like the honeybees," says Michael.

"Do they sting?" I ask.

"No, no," says Michael. "It's that they attack in order to defend their hive—their Home; Adam would fight Death to spare Eve and the children; Eve would offer herself in the delusion that her offering would satisfy God and spare Adam."

"Is that what you want, God?" I ask, frowning. "'Might makes right' and human sacrifice?"

"No, no." God answers. "Of course not. Michael said it was a delusion, didn't he? The behaviors of Adam and Eve indicate that they continue to be immature and willful. If Time allows and they develop more experience, we hope their future decisions will reflect growth and maturity, but of course, they will be able to do so only if they can avoid a premature meeting with Death."

"But they, like I, have now experienced evil," I point out.

"Yes, and it is our hope," God says, "that they will, as they mature, turn that evil into good, as you have done by repudiating Satan and coming Home, or at least to Eden."

"Motherlove," adds Raphael softly, and the other angels nod.

"And honeybee love, as well," adds Michael.

I look at Death, whose form and features continue to transform: smoother flesh, cheekbones, eyelashes sheltering eyes whose bony ridges have softened, a nose instead of a beak, lips that frame a mouth and not a maw. Sleeping, he could now be taken for one of God's children.

And yet...

"God, you know that, as Satan's son, Death may be forever drawn to evil, forever limited to experiencing nothing beyond his appetite and desires."

"Yes, we do know that," God answers. "But as Satan's daughter, you have demonstrated that such is not always the case. You have certainly grown and changed as you repudiated the evil that is your father. This change may be possible for Death as well, unless he's capable only of appetite, in which case he cannot exercise choice anymore than can Shark when he sends Squid on a journey of rebirth."

"This rebirth, God," I say, as the genesis of an idea forms. "How does it work in Time?"

"Eden's children are born, grow, mature, and age in Time, and then are recycled through rebirth. Matter and energy are continually transformed but their essential nature remains constant."

"Constant? Or static?" I ask. Gabriel lifts his wings in interest.

"What's the difference?" Raphael asks.

"If Adam and Eve had matured and been reborn rather than committing themselves to Death, how would they have been reborn?"

"As Adam and Eve, naturally," answers Raphael. "As themselves."

"As themselves, would they repeat the circumstances that occurred during this birth and eventually curse themselves to Death, since that is what will have already happened?"

"Perhaps," says Raphael, less certainly than before.

"It always remains their choice, their free choice," says God.

"But if their natures are static, or even constant," I say, "then how would their set of choices be any different? Why wouldn't they simply recycle their behaviors?"

"They might," God replies. "They can. That is the nature of free will."

"But what will happen now that they are going to meet Death?" I ask.

"They will cease to exist, just as the creatures Death has already devoured have ceased to exist. We would create more children who would not be Adam and Eve."

"And we will miss them," add the angels. "They are our much beloved children."

We are all silent as we think about the loss of Adam and Eve.

"It seems as though Satan triumphs if he continues as an immortal but Adam and Eve meet Death," I say. "So, what about Satan? What other moves will he make in this cruel game he's playing?"

"The better question is 'What other moves *can* he make in this cruel game he *has played*?' answers God. "Satan to this point has not grown. He has only inflated. When he stepped away and unleashed Time's force, that separation revealed you, whom we know to be Time's daughter as well as Satan's better part. Since, so far, he has shown himself incapable of growth, what's left of him will decay in Time. Part of him lives on in you, in Death, and in his seven misbegotten offspring, the Sins, but as for Satan himself, he *was* Lucifer Light Bringer, our bright light; he *is* manifest evil, swollen with pride, greed, and envy; he *will* be simply a windy bag of gases."

"Are you cursing Satan?" I ask. "Damning him?"

"We don't damn anyone, including Satan," God says. "Why would we call evil down upon anyone, even him, when our purpose is not to further separate us but to bring us all, all back Home?

"But Satan has damned himself, and when we say that Satan will be a windy bag of gases, we acknowledge the way in which he continues to call evil down upon himself, even as it leads to deterioration and decay."

"Are Adam and Eve cursed to meet Death?" I ask.

"They are," God says. "They, like Satan, have invoked that curse upon themselves."

"But is a curse always meant to call down evil?" I ask.

"It is the definition of the word 'curse,'" God says solemnly. "And it is an action of free will, like choosing to separate or choosing to eat the Fruit of the Knowledge of Good and Evil after being warned not to."

"So a curse turns Time from what could be to what will be, eliminating the possibilities for growth and change," I muse. God does not disagree. "But why was the fruit forbidden in the first place?" I ask.

God sighs. "We suspected that Adam and Eve were not ready. Had they waited, in good Time they would have matured sufficiently to be able to assimilate the knowledge without bodily incorporating the evil along with the good.

Really, God? You'd place a deadly object in reach of your curious and impulsive children and then tell them not to touch it? How very peculiar. Is it possible, God, that you are still feeling your way around change and growth and Time yourself? Then, of course, I realize that this is not the moment to introduce a discussion of parenting styles.

"It wasn't the fruit that was unripe; it was the children," I offer instead.

"Yes," God answers. "These children who are born in Time—both yours and ours, but particularly ours—experience Time very differently from elementals."

"Not being an elemental myself," I say, "perhaps I can understand more easily their perspective."

"Perspective?" asks God.

"Perspective. The point from which they view events. Elementals can see what was, is, and *what shall be*. Children in Time see only what was and is. Their vantage point, their perspective, is therefore different. It's as if elementals can see the whole of Eden spread out like a grand tapestry, whereas children in Time are confined to living in the warp and woof of that tapestry."

God nods. "Continue."

"It seems to me that our children, born in Time, are themselves far more impulsive than their parents." I hesitate here for a second, or a moment. "And by impulsive, I mean far more responsive to the 'pulse' of Time—that they would act 'in the moment' of each pulse. This is part of the plan of your creation, is it not? That they would live more in the moment?"

God nods again, and the other angels nod with him. I look at my son Death, whose eyes and limbs twitch with the dreams, experiences, and expectations of fresh food and fresh air. "So Adam, Eve, and Death, all children born in Time, all act impulsively." More nods. "Death was born of Satan, of evil, and Adam and Eve have incorporated evil by eating the fruits of the Tree of Knowledge of Good and Evil. But incorporated evil is not necessarily evil embodied," I continue. "You have already acknowledged that these children, along with myself and Death, have also incorporated good, that we are a mixture. Perhaps that is true for all of us, even the elementals." God and the angels become still and stiff. Michael's sword manifests. I realize once more that this is not a good Time to speak about the mixed nature of God's past decisions, so I speak to future possibilities instead.

"Can we all come Home, even Death?"

"We want all children to be able to come Home, yes," God confirms. "Except for Death. He is not compatible with immortality."

Here I go. Now or never. "But he can be the catalyst for freeing mortal children of Time's impulsivity, which apparently is a potential curse as well as a potential blessing."

"That is so," agrees God.

"And, Death is also not evil," I say. "At least not entirely so. You yourself have said so. Nor are Adam and Eve."

Michael has looked anxious during this exchange. How can all this discussion lead to a conclusion of the story that lets everyone come Home? But God nods in understanding. So, accordingly, do the angels.

"You have revealed our path. We will incorporate Death at the end of each child's life cycle," God announces. "That is how we will free each child of the limited and limiting perspectives of Time. At the end of Time, at least for each child, Death will take the body, feed on it, and recycle it, much the way our Edenic children used to do."

We observe the rats, dogs, hyenas, and eagles that already feed in Death's vicinity, *grazing like little deaths, conferring indignity after indignity upon the once-living.* "Not so different from the way in which Shark feeds on Squid," Raphael points out.

Or Death fed on his Hellborn siblings.

"Not so different," God agrees. "But the essential singular element of the child, the *psyche* of the child can come Home to us, should it choose to do so, just as you have come Home to us, Daughter of Satan and Time. Thus, Death becomes part of our plan to bring good out of evil. Although Death's father is Satan, his mother is you, Sin, which means Death carries the potential for good. Our Edenic children will no longer be reborn as themselves; they will evolve—or devolve, or both—into new creatures with unique psyches.

'Psyche,' a younger sibling to matter and energy, and perhaps a way to reconcile some differences with the Greek side of the family. The Author gets to change the storyline after all, and now Death has found a place in this ruined but still vibrant land. More than I'd dared hope, a place for my son. But I keep my happiness in check as I consider what this implies for the children of Eden. "I must say that, as Death's mother, I know my son's impulsive nature," I respond. "And incorporating him will certainly make the cycle more volatile. Children's journeys may and will be interrupted or extended in unTimely ways."

"Yes, that is so," answers God. "And their journeys may be filled with more pain and strife, as well as more experience. But their natures will no longer be static."

Static. Fixed and stationary. Immovable. Like the dull sameness of the gatekeeper. Still, the gatekeeper is safer than the explorer, who chooses experience over security. I alone here have experienced both. Shall I leave these elementals to their nostalgia for a simpler past? Or is it Time to move on? Will choice be about being or becoming?

God looks at me as if they know what I am thinking. *Very well then.*

I clear my throat. "Change carries risk. It may be, that having met Death, the newer children will be born with varying degrees of incorporated good and evil, that some will change through family love; that some will respond to their own experiences of the good or evil in themselves or others without ever connecting those experiences to any Homecoming; that some will respond only to appetite without ever recognizing it as the desire to come Home. These children may well manifest more good or more evil themselves, and, God, some of it may well even be done in your name."

"We know," says God. "It may be, too, that parents, knowing that they themselves will meet Death, will love their children and plan *what could be* for them rather than *what is* for themselves."

Or they could become envious of their children's lives and, afraid that there is no Home, will seek to extend their own lives at their children's expense. Or they could attempt to amass earthly power in anticipation of buying their way Home. Or they could kill and eat each other. Or… Or… Or…. A tear rolls down my cheek at the thought that the children of Eden *could be* capable of more evil than Satan himself. Raphael gently wipes the tear away.

"We know," God says. "We understand. And that, too, will be the choice of Adam and Eve's children.

"But let us now speak of a more joyous event. Sin, you were born of Satan and you are the original sign of separation from the wholeness and unity that was once We. But you were also born of Time. You separated yourself from your evil author, and your experience in doing so and the actions you've taken as a result of that experience could save many of our children, including Adam and Eve, from prematurely meeting Death. In addition to being the original

sign of separation, you are also the original sign of reconcil-
iation and reunion. It is Time to signify that change. Your
name is no longer Sin, but Wisdom."

"Welcome Home, Wisdom!" chorus the angels.

*Hmmmm. All well and good, as if a name change undoes
the past. But that's not how Time works. I'm still me, aren't
I? And, God, if I had remained the unchanged dutiful child of
Satan as you'd expected, Death and I would still be stewing in
our own wastes, waiting for either you or Satan to change your
mind. But would you have, God? Would you have changed if I
hadn't chosen to become instead of to be? I changed my life. You
changed your mind, and then you changed my name. But what's
in a name, anyway?* I wipe yet another tear away. *No sense
looking backward. It's not about where we started once upon a
Time, or where we will be tomorrow, whenever tomorrow will
be. It's about where we are now. Here, now. In this moment.*

Home.

Family, such as it is.

"Well." I clear my throat. "That's done then." I look at
Death as I collect my thoughts. He frowns in his sleep,
revealing a dimple. "That's done then," I repeat. "But we're
not, are we? Death will soon be ready for his next meal."

"Yes," says God. "And now you must excuse us, Wisdom, while we consider judgment for our children." They
shimmer and disembody. Death stirs.

*What's this? Left alone with Death again? So now I'm fam-
ily, but I'm still not included in their deliberations. Judgment
without Wisdom, Really?*

Facing Judgment

Eden continued to age. The trees and plants withered; a boreal gust replaced the balmy zephyr. Adam and Eve set their faces into the wind, sensing that Death lay in wait at the source. They wrapped themselves in more fig leaves against the cold, but the chill permeated. They moved quickly, even against the wind, as if slowing down would give them too much Time to reconsider.

The wind brought the smell of Death, of cadaverines and putrescenes. *A familiar, still homely sort of smell for me, but I can see the fear in their eyes as they pinch their nostrils against the stench.*

Soon Adam and Eve saw the broad path harrowed by Death, along with the remnants of the children Death had already taken. As far ahead as they could see, bones and the occasional skull, fur, feathers, boulders, leaves, splinters, and mounds of earth lined the path, as if the way to Death were not already plain enough to follow.

"Are those the footprints of Death?" Adam asked, pointing to two nearby lakes from which geysers of steam and sulfur rose.

"What mighty claws he must have!" said Eve, looking at a small mountain of dirt and boulders and the ragged trenches beyond that led to a massive, freshly dug pit.

"And what giant teeth!" Adam added, gazing at the gnawed and clawed remains of a once-towering hemlock.

When they discovered the hide and a few of the bones of Brown Bear, they marveled at how such a massive child could be emptied out and tossed away like a discarded husk of corn. "This, too, must be Death's work," they told each other. When Adam saw that Eve now shivered with cold as well as fear, he stood awhile in thought. Then, murmuring his apologies to Bear for disturbing his skin, Adam split the thick furry hide and made warming cloaks for Eve and himself. When he draped Eve's over her head and around her shoulders, she all but disappeared under the coarse fur, leaving only a small human face with frightened eyes and a runny nose. He donned his own. They regarded each other, bundled in Bear and wearing another child's smell. Now they were less human, but they were warmer. Not knowing what else to say or do, they thanked God and Bear for the gift and trudged on as the cloaks draggled along in the dust, sweeping away their human footprints.

━

It's Time. I leave my drowsing son to meet them.

━

I stepped into their path.

They stopped.

"Are you Death?" asked Adam. "You're not how I thought you'd look."

"And are you Adam and Eve, or are you Bear children?" I asked. "You're not how I thought you'd look, either."

Adam growled, "I thought you'd be as big as a cedar with fangs the size of mountaintops. Why, you're no bigger than Eve."

"I am not Death, but I am Death's mother," I responded. "He is my son."

Adam stood up to his full height and puffed out his chest. "Well, then, I am not afraid of your son Death!" he said.

"Oh, but you should be," I responded.

He raised both his fists. "Let Death come," Adam roared. "And we'll see who is the mightier."

I see already. Wearing Bear's toughness like a cloak. Self-deluded as well as self-absorbed, but radiant even in fear, defiance, and trembling. I can understand why Satan wanted to turn them. "Silly boy!" I said. "You've seen the bones—grander bones than yours—of the other children's remains. What makes you think yourself mightier than they were?"

Adam stood momentarily speechless, no doubt working up some sort of response to this entirely rhetorical question, but as he did so, Eve, she who God says is too quiet and shy to speak up, spoke up. "Death is your child? You are his mother?"

"I am," I admitted.

"I will be a mother as well, if Death spares us for a Time," she said.

"I know," I responded. "And I stand here, for a Time at least, to help you do that."

"Why would Death's mother help us?" Adam demanded.

"Before we find ourselves arguing instead of helping each other," I said, "Let's all introduce ourselves. I know that you are God's children, Adam and Eve, yes?"

Adam nodded. "How did you know our names before we told you?" Eve asked.

"God and I have been discussing how to make good come out of the evil that came from deciding to eat of the fruit of the Tree of Knowledge of Good and Evil. You called up Death, my son, and now it looks as though you're rushing to meet him. We want you to reconsider."

"Why would Death's mother want us to reconsider meeting Death?" asked Adam.

Annoying child. I have a name. "And the reason that I wanted to make introductions is so that you will know that

I too have a name, that I am not simply 'Death's mother.' My name is Wisdom."

"'Wisdom' is a beautiful name," said Eve. "'Adam' means Man and 'Eve' means Woman. What does 'Wisdom' mean?"

"It's not a name I have designated," added Adam.

"'Wisdom' is the perception of good informed by Time, experience, and knowledge—of maturity, one could say," I said. "Adam, are not 'Man' and 'Woman' both designations of maturity?"

"Well, yes," Adam said.

"In rushing toward Death you demonstrate your ongoing immaturity. Then how have you earned the designations of Man and Woman?"

Adam looked uncomfortable but remained silent. Eve smiled ruefully. "Perhaps Adam will have to give us new names, if we don't run out of Time first."

"Perhaps that won't be necessary," I said. "I was born of evil, the shadow daughter of what you, Adam, called the 'dark monster' in the garden." Adam took a step back and drew Eve closer to his side. "Oh, he was real. And still is." I sighed. "Like you, I was only a child, but unlike you, I had my own child—Death—to raise. And my father the monster abandoned both of us. But there were others who helped me learn to care for myself and my son. And I acquired the knowledge over Time—experience—to realize that I could leave evil and choose good. And I choose to use that experience to help you the way I was helped. If you will let me."

Eve nodded. After a moment, Adam did also.

"You, the children of God, were born of good and lovingly nurtured. But my father convinced you to taste the knowledge of evil, to incorporate it along with the good.

Now you are experiencing its aftertaste. What is the knowledge that you have gained from this experience?"

Adam and Eve murmured to each other and then turned to me. "That we know both good and evil."

Merely introduced, I'm afraid, but at least that's a start.

"That we know pain."

Again, merely introduced, but perhaps pleasure will be the sweeter because of it.

"And we know loneliness, even though we have each other."

Ah, here it is at last, the loneliness that leads to the desire for Homecoming. "You also have God," I said.

"They have turned away from us and left us to battle Death on our own," Adam said.

"Why would you say that?" I asked. "You've turned away from them. God has not turned away from you. I'm here on their behalf, as well as my own."

"We haven't seen God, nor have we heard any angel songs since the day after we ate the fruit," Eve said.

"It was you, not God, who hid in the Garden." *Are they ready to hear what I must say? Are they ready to listen and choose?* "In your ignorance, you assumed that what you saw and heard in the moment of eating the fruit was all there was to see and hear.

"And then you assumed that there was some fabulous knowledge in the fruit.

"And then you assumed that you could snatch that knowledge from your other self.

"And then you assumed that you could rely entirely on each other to fix this mess.

"What do your experience and knowledge tell you now?"

Adam shook his head violently at each of these statements, as if they were slaps to his certainties. Eve looked at me with agonized eyes. No one had previously spoken to Adam like this.

"That we left God, that they didn't leave us?"

"That God is still there for us?"

"That we are still their children?"

"Yes, yes, and yes," I replied.

"That we don't have to meet Death?"

"No," I responded. "You still have to meet Death. But not now, unless you persist along this path. And there's an additional responsibility that you've taken on by eating the fruit of the Knowledge of Good and Evil. When you knew only good, you loved God in the innocence of bliss. Now you must choose to love. Your experience has replaced your innocence. However, you also have Time, good Time, if you use it wisely and patiently, to make that choice. And I, Wisdom, promise to join you, if you'll have me, on your journey to judgment and Death."

All right, God, I've done what I can. The rest is up to Adam and Eve. And you, of course.

I appreciate how negotiating a collective of voices into a singular authority can be complicated, not to say difficult. The primordials have shown you that, if nothing else. But even the most original story can benefit from fresh perspectives. If I were allowed an editorial comment, I would say that giving the children judgment rather than more Time to mature will create unnecessary plot complications. I know, I know. We already had that discussion, and you as Author have apparently already made your decision. But there's always Time to reconsider, God. To change your mind. You have that choice.

I sigh. "Are you ready?" I asked Adam and Eve.

They nodded.

I nodded as well. "We're ready."

Adam and Eve hear God's judgment without seeing God's countenance, which is too formidable for them to bear at this moment. Their disobedience weighs heavily; their heads bend in shame; they gaze at the ground. "They're just children!" I want to say, but wait silently with them. I alone study God's faces, dark with disapproval and foreboding.

First God pronounces judgment on the snake, lack of habeas corpus notwithstanding. "Cursed are you above all other animals. On your belly you will go, you will eat dust, and Eve and her daughters will hate you, and you them."

I blink. *What is this? Why curse the snake, who was either forced or seduced by Satan into giving over his body? By the way, where is that snake, anyway? How did he manage to wriggle out of this confrontation?* I tremble for what comes next.

Next, God speaks to Eve. "You will bear children in pain and sorrow, your desire shall be for Adam, and he will rule over you."

I shake with distress on Eve's behalf. *What? As the mother of one monster and countless monster meals, I can speak with some authority regarding pain and sorrow in childbirth. I cannot recommend either of them.*

And why, Oh God, why on Earth would you want to make Eve subject to Adam? You created them with complementary personalities, but now, in the same way that Eden was tipped out of equilibrium, you are tipping their relationship. And do you really think that Adam, let alone Eve, benefits from "ruling" Eve, from telling her what to do and how to do it? I clench my hands to keep them from shaking.

Third, God speaks to Adam. "Cursed be the soil for your sake. You will toil to take food from it until you return to the soil yourself. You are dust, and to dust you shall return."

And now I shake with anger on Adam's behalf. *You cursed the ground! You called down evil upon it! Why would you call down evil into your beautiful Eden? And why more toil when what Adam needs is more Time to play?*

Pain.

Sorrow.

Inequality.

Toil.

Dust.

Death.

Stripped of innocence and childhood, Adam and Eve, in bewildered obedience, move in the direction God has indicated, away from their home, away from Death—for the moment—and toward adulthood.

I follow, as bewildered as they. Can there be Authority without Wisdom? *When God gave themself away to their children, did they also give away their common sense? Maybe I'll understand the ways of God some Time, even if I can't justify them. But not here. Not now. Not this Time.*

One More Bedtime Story

Death considers his next meal: the sky-blue speckled egg of a roc, whose very large and angry mother swoops down on him again and again and tries to peck out his eyes. *Motherlove*. He flicks his pinions, creating an updraft that spins her away. Now that he's sure he has enough food for his boundless appetite, he's starting to discriminate between dirt and dog, rock and roc. I'm encouraged. But he still doesn't speak. He plucks the egg from its nest and pops it into his mouth as if it were a blueberry and swallows it whole. "If you chew an egg, you can taste its inside as well as its outside," I say.

A shimmer teases the edge of my vision. Thinking that it's the mother coming back to scold my son, I turn to commiserate with her on her loss. Instead, I see Raphael slowly manifesting, as if unsure of its welcome. "You think God was harsh in their judgment of Adam and Eve," the angel says.

I frown. "Damn right I do," I mutter.

Raphael smiles. "Now, now. You didn't like it when God cursed the ground and Adam. So why would you curse 'right'?"

"Figure of speech," I sigh. "Ask one of the Muses."

"Actually, I did."

"'Right/Wrong.' 'Correct/Incorrect.' 'Good/Evil.' Make a judgment and choose sides."

Raphael doesn't argue. Instead it nods at Death, who frowns and inspects the now-empty nest. "We've been thinking about eggs," Raphael says to Death.

"We?" I ask, looking around to see who else has manifested.

"I am here on behalf of many of us."

I nod. "Go on."

"We've been considering the difference between their outsides and insides."

"As have we," I say. My son, watching me, grabs a clutch of dodo eggs and pops them into his mouth. I raise my eyebrows, and he crunches down. Yellow yolks spurt out the sides of his mouth. "Chew with your mouth closed," I advise.

"Yes, well," Raphael continues. "Before Time, We sang with joy about the smooth and seamless shell created by the harmony between its shape and texture. It was so beautiful, so right." I nod. "We could have contemplated that shell for eternity.

"But then the egg cracked." Raphael says this solemnly. Death looks up.

"It's the only way to free the contents," I respond.

"And so the cosmos began. As it happens, at the Time we ourselves were all very young. And inexperienced."

I wait for more, but Raphael stays silent. We watch Death poke a turtle who has withdrawn into her shell, wisely refusing to expose herself. After a moment, Death turns his attention to a skittery newt. "Is that an apology you're offering?" I finally ask.

"God doesn't apologize," answers Raphael. Death, gazing hungrily, sidles toward the angel. "But perhaps we learn, just like Death here."

I frown again. "He doesn't speak," I say. "How would we know whether he learns?"

Raphael rustles its soft pinions around Death. "You know, I used to tell stories to Eden's children before they left the Nest. Adam and Eve enjoyed them. Perhaps Death will, too. May I?"

"If you wish," I say.

"I call this story 'The Vanishing Serpent in Eden.'

"Once a wandering woman wondered why, when—"

"Stop right there," I say. "How much more alliteration do you plan to practice in this story?"

"You don't like alliteration? You don't think it's fun?"

"Maybe, but only in small doses, like limericks. And by the way, please don't even think about using limericks; we've heard more than enough of them already."

Raphael nods, thinks for a moment, and begins again. "There was a Time when Sin believed that God was too harsh in their judgment of Adam and Eve but not harsh enough in their judgment of Satan, that God had mistakenly cursed the snake instead of the monster."

"Wait," I say. "Are you providing enough exposition for your listeners?"

Raphael frowns. "You and Death are my listeners. What more exposition do either of you need?" I nod, conceding the point. Death watches us with wide eyes. "Now do I have your permission to continue?" the angel asks grandly.

"If you—"

"—Without interruption?"

I purse my lips. "Very well."

"It is midday in Eden. A beautiful but insecure and immature Eve is alone following an argument with Adam, her other self. She is hot, sweaty, tired, thirsty, and reconsidering whether it was wise to work alone.

"Enter a strange but handsome powerful, sinuous, provocative male transformed into a talking Serpent who professes that he, unlike Adam, is wholly and completely at

Eve's service, that he understands her better than anyone else, that he adores her."

"Not very funny," I think to myself and shake my head. Raphael stops. Death touches my shoulder and frowns. I nod for the angel to continue.

"Now Eve may be credulous, but she's certainly not stupid, and she's quite curious to know how it is that the Serpent speaks to her in her own language, and when she catches him in a contradiction, the Awesomely Artful Artificer—" I hold up my hand. Raphael stops and edits itself. "And when she catches him in a contradiction, the Artificer must flatter and misdirect her until she falls foil to his flummery, dupe to his deception, prey to his prestidigitation." Raphael stops once more, daring me to interrupt. I open my mouth to speak, then shrug. It's the angel's story, not mine. Mouth open in admiration, Death stares at Raphael, who looks smug.

"Please do continue," I say.

"Well, then, enough enconiums to misdirection and legerdemain. To summarize, Adam and Eve fall from favor, get kicked out of the Garden, are counseled by Wisdom, judged by God, and prepared for Death." Here Raphael nods in our direction, and we nod back. *Does Death know he's inside this story?*

"Alas, Satan's performance goes unappreciated in Eden. In fact, according to his critics, it's damnably awful, and so he decides to return to where he'll be appreciated: to his famously infernal faithful fiends.

"But events don't go as planned this Time. First, there's the great physical weariness of flapping his way back to Hell on wings that barely seem to carry his weight, so stiff and out of shape are they from the effort of inhabiting the body of the Seductive Serpent. In fact, he feels stiff and out of shape all over, as if he's holding a great tiredness at bay. That's the cost, he consoles himself, of such a bravura once-in-a-lifeTime performance.

"Ahh, the drama of drama.

"So our Vanishing Serpent summons the remains of his energy. 'Just one more performance, one farewell tour,' Satan thinks to himself, and then he can rest all he wants. Once he's recovered his strength, maybe he'll take a nice vacation in Eden, pick up some distressed real estate. There should be plenty to choose from. After all, his boy Death has been busy deconstructing the neighborhood, just the way Satan has deconstructed God's narrative."

Death blinks at this linking of Death and Satan, as if his father is here with us in the Garden instead of protectively caged inside the story.

"Too bad, Satan thinks, that the lad hasn't inherited his old man's sparkle, but, really, Death is history."

Death vigorously flaps his wings in denial, generating a cyclone on a nearby island that levels its bamboo forest, exposing a feeding rat who is snatched by a migrating hawk who eats, digests, and then voids the rat's remains on a far-away continent where a new bamboo forest springs up, attracting gorillas, pandas, lemurs, and more rats. I enfold Death in a hug. Gradually his wings settle and he stops shivering.

The air settles as well. Raphael resumes. "Satan decides that it's the seven little deadlies who will keep Adam and Eve busy for the rest of their miserable lives. Death can feed on the remains." Death clenches his jaw but remains still. Raphael raises an eyebrow at me. I nod for him to continue. "The traffic in Chaos is muddled, as usual. Matter and energy transform in a frenzy of activity: quarks, particles, strings, and streams collide with no deference for

Satan's presence. Rude, but what can be expected with such a disarray? Satan swears that, after this final performance, he'll never put up with this kind of anarchy again. Yes, he'll retire to a cozy nest near his new children in what's left of Eden and watch the little deadlies (and maybe some grandchildren, littler venials) make him proud.

"The gates of Hell stand open. Why shouldn't they? Where Death and his mother once sat is an abandoned dump. Just as well.

"Hell is darker than Satan remembers, or maybe it's just that his darkness is less visible. No matter. Less energy. Chaos was exhausting.

"One last performance. Then he's done. He squares his wings and enters the theater. So what if the stage is dark? The footlights await. And so does his audience. On with the Show!

"No stage manager assists, so he has to find his own mark in the dim cavern. The spotlight hits. Satan blinks against its glare. The harsh light blinds him, but he can hear the rustling and sibilant whispers of his audience, his fiends and family. He wishes he could see their expressions, but, no matter. The show will go on.

"He enters, covered in glory.

"But his audience can't see the glory, the glare being so harsh and all. Someone really should speak to the stage manager, but who?

"Oh yes, the show must go on. Satan's noble brow shiny with effort, or maybe it's only sweat, his limbs twitching with effort, he speaks: 'Fiends and Hellspawn, Once again I've returned in triumph, this Time with the news-s that, thank-s be all to me, the gates-s of Hell are wide open and the path to Eden is-s clearly marked for you to follow.'

"He pauses for applause, but the audience fails to take its cue.

"'Provincials.' he snarls to himself.

"But then Satan remembers who he is. And where he is. And what he's owed. In the effort of a lifetime, he resumes. 'Plunged into the horrors of Chaos and the forces of God, I s-s-aw s-s-s-ights that would s-s-s-end a le-s-s-s-s-s doughty warrior shrieking back to the s-s-s-s-safety of Hell.'

"The rustling in the audience grows louder as Satan stutters his sibilants. What's the matter? Are his fiends holding any grudges from Satan's previous tour when he introduced them to broadscale drunkenness, mayhem, mutilation, and cannibalism? But how should any of that affect their appreciation for his current triumphal tour? After all, ars longa, vita brevis."

"Unless, of course, you're an immortal." I say. *Give Death his due.*

Raphael nods. "But Satan looks old and sounds tired. He hisses as if his teeth don't fit. His message is old and tired, too. The audience has heard most of it before. As he continues to age before their very eyes, they mock him with sibilant hissing. He withers and shrinks. Finally, stiff with exhaustion, he drops to his knees and struggles with his lines: 'But I prevailed! Even though God knows-s-s-s that it was-s I who brought Eve and Adam to ruin, they have curs-s-s-ed the s-s-s-s-snake ins-s-s-s-s-s-tead of me! Is-s-s-n't that marvelous-s-s-s-s-s, Fellow Fiends-s-s-s-ss and Friends-s-s-s-sss?! Curs-s-s-ing the s-s-s-s-snake ins-s-s-s-s-tead of me?'

"But the hissing only increases.

"The footlights dim, the house lights come up.

"Satan shades his eyes to better see into the seats, but there are no seats.

"Only the pit.

"In the pit slither adders and asps; black snakes and boas; catsnakes, copperheads, and cobras; garters and grass snakes; hognose and hoop snakes; keelback and kings; mambas and moccasins; pine snakes and pythons; racers, rats, and rattlers; sidewinders and striped snakes; vipers and watersnakes, just to name a few.

"The rattlers shake their tails until the pit itself vibrates.

"It's too much, even for the Fiend of FlimFlam.

"Already on his knees, Satan falls prone and slithers into the pit.

"Boo!

"His-s-s-ss-s-ss!"

I laugh and clap as Raphael beams and takes a bow. "Wonderful story!" I say. "Who could ask for a better ending, other than Satan, of course. 'Boo! His-s-s-s!' indeed!"

"Hi-s-s-s—s-s," says Death. Raphael and I both turn and stare. Death beams and says again, "Hi-s-s-s-ss-s!"

My boy is growing up. What will I do with myself when he doesn't need me anymore?

Becoming Like One of Us

"Now that the humans have become like one of us, knowing good and evil, they may well reach out and take from the Tree of Life and live forever," God says.

There's a tree of life that's an antidote for Death? "I don't understand, God," I say. "I don't want to sound ungrateful, but why would you let Death into the Garden if Adam and Eve could live forever by eating from a tree that wasn't even prohibited to them?"

"It did not seem necessary when Adam and Eve were innocently good, but now that they know both, if they think they can live forever, they may never choose between the two. That is why Eden is no longer open to them." God adds, "The choice they must make about whether their psyches come Home to us is part of their possibility for growth."

"But not part of yours?" I ask, directing my question to the elementals. Feathers rustle as they simultaneously shrug their shoulders. "I see," I say slowly, "that it must be another matter of Time. Where is this tree, anyway?"

"Right next to the Tree of the Knowledge of Good and Evil," Raphael responds, now looking less angelic, even less birdlike. Sheepish, in fact.

How can anyone imagine ever justifying the ways of God to Man, let alone Woman or Wisdom? "Hiding in plain sight," I say. "Good and evil. GOoD and dEvil."

"Yes. What was originally the strife between elementals has now been internalized within the humans themselves,"

God responds. "They carry it around within them wherever they go, just as Satan carries Hell with him always."

"Can we help them with this strife?" Raphael asks.

"Yes," adds Michael, the archangel who continues to polish his sword against real and imaginary foes, whose sense of family made him once upon a Time an advocate for separation from all who were not of the original elementals. "Can we help them with this strife, this battle?" He ducks his head into his breast feathers for a moment, but then looks directly at me. "I say this as one whose pride in my own lineage and prowess blinded me to see the good in others. I say this as one who can therefore understand the way in which pride can burrow into human marrow.

"I say this as one who will help them, if I can, to fight their inner demons and outer foes."

And Gabriel adds, "I will give them the languages and rhythms of music to regulate, stimulate, or quiet their natural impulses, as they choose."

"Perhaps I can teach Adam and Eve patience in the face of impulsivity," Raphael says.

"How would you approach them, Raphael?" God asks.

"I would tell them another, younger story of 'Once Upon a Time,'" Raphael answers.

"Would the 'Time' in 'Upon a Time' be GOoD or dEvil?" God asks.

And here Raphael covers its face with its wings and remains silent. Then it shakes its head from side to side: once, twice, three Times.

"Maybe a little of both," I offer.

"Raphael, you will confer upon them healing, great healing, with your love and compassion," says God.

We wait for Raphael to recover its composure.

"These children are gendered, as am I, along with some of you," I say. "But you chose; we didn't. One immediate and perceptible effect of eating the fruit was to amplify their perception of sexual difference." *Satan may have first uttered the trope of she as a shadow he, but, God, you magnified it when you cursed Eve.* "Perhaps I can help mediate some of those perceptions."

"In our next Creation," God adds, darkly, "We will either eliminate gender and sexuality or make it varied like the color and textures of hair, eye, or skin. This bifurcation of good versus evil, us versus them, and now male versus female is an unnecessary complication."

But, God, it was you who made this about "versus." And you applied it only to your human children, not to the snakes and lizards, fish and frogs, birds and beasts who continue to play freely among the fields of gender and sexuality. You allowed your other children to mature and start their own families, to go their independent ways. But you kept Adam and Eve bound to you by the rules of a motherlove so restrictive—obedience versus independence, innocence versus experience, GOoD versus dEvil—that the only way they could break that bond was to choose each other over you. And so they did. And then of course you felt betrayed, first by flighty Eve, then by your good boy Adam. Any parent would. So you punished them. What's done is done. But now, let them go until you and they can grow together again in the fullness of Time. Let them find their own way Home. That is what I think.

But, God, I also believe that you yourself are still quite young, that you're hiding your own hurt behind the mask of judgment, so this is what I say instead: "But wouldn't it be a great experiential exercise in growth for the children themselves, to address those polarities over Time?" I ask. "After all, God, the first polarity came from the elementals and primordials themselves."

"So it did," admits God, and they grow dreamy-eyed. "But what if we create a new world in which polarity is irrelevant?"

Raphael goes dreamy-eyed. "What if in this new world all children thirst for good knowledge only? *And all angels are teachers to obedient and unquestioning students?*

Gabriel grows dreamy-eyed. What if in this new world all children are part of a grand symphony? *All playing the same tune?*

Michael goes dreamy-eyed. "What if the sentient children are all spore-shooters like the fungi?"

But why shoot anything, let alone spores? Where's the pleasure in that? Although, letting the skull of my slingshot fly, hearing its hiss of flight and thwack of contact, watching it hit Death precisely where I'd aimed, the dust flying up as he dropped to the ground.... Come to think of it, maybe there's something to be said for sentient spore shooters. Hmmmm. It's tough being Wisdom when the Sublime is constantly rubbing shoulders with the Silly. "Mm-hmm," I say, nodding my head as if these are all wise thoughts. "Sentient children, you say. In this world, are all the children sentient, or only some of them?"

"Mmmh," says Raphael. "An interesting question."

"Do they all have psyches?"

"Mmmh," says God. "Let us consider that question further."

"And, in this World, the one you've already created as opposed to the worlds that might follow, have you given any thought to reducing the hierarchical relationships among your elementals and your children?"

"What!?" asks Raphael in horror.

"What!?!" echo Gabriel and Michael.

"What!?!!" asks God. "Have you not seen Chaos for yourself, Wisdom? Hierarchal relationships confer Order, and Order confers Harmony, Peace, and Togetherness."

Maybe I'll save this discussion for another day. Or another Time. A Better Time.

SomeTimes the better part of Wisdom is discretion.

At the End of the Day, Relatively Speaking

On this quiet evening, Death and I walk the Earth together. He is still easily distracted by the scent of ebbing life, but he is now a handsome young man with a strong resemblance to Adam when Adam was a lad. Unlike Adam and his descendants, though, Death doesn't have to prove anything.

He walks with Wisdom.

Not that I want to boast about my soothing influence, but, as I've told God, all Death needed was some fresh air and good food, and there's plenty of both in this still blue and thriving world.

Gruff Michael has taken Death under his wing, so to speak, and they do in fact go fishing together: two psyches— *souls*, as God has taken to calling them—in companionable silence, watching the ripples on the pond as trout rise to the bait.

Or not.

It doesn't matter whether they do or not, of course, since the trout will sooner or later come to Death.

Michael is growing into a fine friend. I love him for his kindness and willingness to cross the boundaries between the certainties of what was and the uncertainties of what is and what could be.

Yes, uncertainties.

God still assures us that uncertainties result directly from free will. I continue to question whether free will is equally distributed among the children of Adam and Eve, especially now that Cain, the firstborn of Adam and Eve, has summoned Death to his own brother Abel. I could see Death's confusion in being called by Cain. In the natural course of Time, shouldn't Death have met his parents Adam and Eve before meeting the son?

Cain the firstborn. The first murderer. *Satan may be retired, but certainly the seven little deadlies continue to play hard.*

Raphael was just as baffled as Death by this unTimeliness, and for that, I love Raphael. In fact, I love all the elementals for their adoption of us along with this strange new world. Of course I love God, too, but God, manifest as the collective splendor of the remaining elementals, remains intimidating and, lately, more distant. Maybe we all still have some growing up to do.

I'm curious (another characteristic I share with Adam and Eve and their children) to see, as more souls choose whether or not to come Home to join God, whether the nature of God changes or remains essential.

God may know, but I don't.

When I can force myself to gaze into the radiance of God, I now see a certain diffidence relating to their earthly children, as if this particular creation story is far enough along its narrative arc that it's Time to think about starting another.

That's all right with me.

Oh, and, proud Mother that I am, did I forget to mention that Death has spoken his first word?

"Hope."

About the Author

Susan Lyons has spent much of her life thinking and dreaming about the physics and metaphysics of time: its teleology and dimensionality, its wrinkles and winged chariot, its downright slipperiness. An English major herself, she remains happily married to a physics major. Together they've raised a music major and a double-major in physics and English, all of whom maintain strong opinions about tempo, temporality, and the time-space continuum. She was also lucky enough to spend most of her professional life as Director of Academic Services at the University of Connecticut's Avery Point campus, where she set up tutoring in math, physics, chemistry, and biology, as well as writing and literature.

One semester, Susan was teaching *Paradise Lost* and wondering why Milton was so hard on Eve and Sin. She was also auditing calculus and attempting to figure out what time and tangents had to do with each other. As she chalked onto a pitted blackboard the arc of Satan's fall from Heaven, it occurred to her that it might well have been he who invented calculus as well as other moral knots. Hence the genesis for *Time's Oldest Daughter*, where, finally, Sin gets a word in edgewise.